Peggy Stewart:
Navy Girl at Home

Gabrielle E. Jackson

1st WORLD
LIBRARY
Literary Society

Peggy Stewart: Navy Girl at Home

Gabrielle E. Jackson

© 1st World Library – Literary Society, 2004
PO Box 2211
Fairfield, IA 52556
www.1stworldlibrary.org
First Edition

LCCN: 2004091186

Softcover ISBN: 1-59540-632-8
eBook ISBN: 1-59540-732-4

Purchase *"Peggy Stewart: Navy Girl at Home"*
as a traditional bound book at:
www.1stWorldLibrary.org/purchase.asp?ISBN=1-59540-632-8

1st World Library Literary Society is a nonprofit
organization dedicated to promoting literacy by:

- Creating a free internet library accessible from any
  computer worldwide.
- Hosting writing competitions and offering book
  publishing scholarships.

Readers interested in supporting literacy
through sponsorship, donations or
membership please contact:
literacy@1stworldlibrary.org
Check us out at: www.1stworldlibrary.org

THIS LITTLE STORY OF ANNAPOLIS IS
MOST AFFECTIONATELY INSCRIBED TO

H.W.H.

WHOSE SUNNY SOUL AND CHEERY
VOICE HELPED TO MAKE MANY AN
HOUR HAPPY FOR THE ONE HE CALLED
"LITTLE MOTHER"

CONTENTS

I. SPRINGTIDE..................7

II. THE EMPRESS.................. 19

III. "DADDY NEIL".................. 32

IV. IN OCTOBER'S DAYS.................. 45

V. POLLY HOWLAND..................58

VI. A FRIENDSHIP BEGINS..................70

VII. PEGGY STEWART: CHATELAINE.................. 81

VIII. A SHOCKING DEMONSTRATION OF
    INTEMPERANCE.................. 93

IX. DUNMORE'S LAST CHRISTMAS.................. 107

X. A DOMESTIC EPISODE..................119

XI. PLAYING GOOD SAMARITAN.................. 133

XII. THE SPICE OF PEPPER AND SALT.................. 147

XIII. THE MASQUERADERS' SHOW.................. 158

XIV. OFF FOR NEW LONDON.................. 170

XV. REGATTA DAY.................. 182

XVI. THE RACE..................194

XVII. SHADOWS CAST BEFORE.................. 207

XVIII. YOU'VE SPOILED THEIR TEA PARTY..................218

XIX. BACK AT SEVERNDALE.................. 230

CHAPTER I

SPRINGTIDE

"Peggy, Maggie, Mag, Margaret, Marguerite, Muggins. Hum! Half a dozen of them. Wonder if there are any more? Yes, there's Peggoty and Peg, to say nothing of Margaretta, Gretchen, Meta, Margarita, Keta, Madge. My goodness! Is there any end to my nicknames? I mistrust I'm a very commonplace mortal. I wonder if other girls' names can be twisted around into as many picture puzzles as mine can? What do YOU think about it Shashai!" [Footnote: Shashai. Hebrew for noble, pronounced Shash'a-ai.] and the girl reached up both arms to draw down into their embrace the silky head of a superb young colt which stood close beside her; a creature which would have made any horse-lover stop stock-still and exclaim at sight of him. He was a magnificent two-year-old Kentuckian, fault-less as to his points, with a head to set an artist rhapsodizing and a-tingle to put it upon his canvas. His coat, mane and tail were black as midnight and glossy as satin. The great, lustrous eyes held a living fire, the delicate nostrils were a-quiver every moment, the faultlessly curved ears alert as a wild creature's. And he WAS half wild, for never had saddle rested upon his back, girth encircled him or bit fretted the sensitive mouth. A halter thus far in his career had been his only badge of bondage and the girl caressing him had beenthe one to put it upon him. It would have been a bad quarter of an hour for any other person attempting it. But she was his "familiar," though far from being his evil genius. On the contrary, she was his presiding spirit of good.

Just now, as the splendid head nestled confidingly in her circling arms, she was whispering softly into one velvety ear, oh, so velvety! as it rested against her ripe, red lips, so soft, so perfect in their molding. The ear moved slightly back and forth, speaking its silent language. The nostrils emitted the faintest bubbling acknowledgment of the whispered words. The beautiful eyes were so expressive in their intelligent comprehension.

"Too many cooks spoil the broth, Shashai. Too many grooms can spoil a colt. Too many mistresses turn a household topsy-turvy. How about too many names, old boy? Can they spoil a girl? But maybe I'm spoiled already. How about it?" and a musical laugh floated out from between the pretty lips.

The colt raised his head, whinnied aloud as though in denial and stamped one deer-like, unshod fore-hoof as though to emphasize his protest; then he again slid his head back into the arms as if their slender roundness encompassed all his little world.

"You old dear!" exclaimed the girl softly, adding: "Eh, but it's a beautiful world! A wonderful world," and broke into the lilting refrain of "Wonderful world" and sang it through in a voice of singularly, haunting sweetness. But the words were not those of the popular song. They had been written and set to its air by Peggy's tutor.

Gabrielle E. Jackson

She seemed to forget everything else, though she continued to mechanically run light, sensitive fingers down the velvety muzzle so close to her face, and semi-consciously reach forth the other hand to caress the head of a superb wolfhound which, upon the first sweet notes, had risen from where she lay not far off to listen, thrusting an insinuating nose under her arm. She seemed to float away with her song, off, off across the sloping, greening fields to the broad, blue reaches of Bound Bay, all a-glitter in the morning sunlight.

She was seated in the crotch of a snake-fence running parallel with the road which ended in a curve toward the east and vanished in a thin-drawn perspective toward the west. There was no habitation, or sign of human being near. The soft March wind, with its thousand earthy odors and promises of a Maryland springtide, swept across the bay, stirring her dark hair, brushed up from her forehead in a natural, wavy pompadour, and secured by a barrette and a big bow of dark red ribbon, the long braid falling down her back tied by another bow of the same color. The forehead was broad and exceptionally intellectual. The eyebrows, matching the dark hair, perfectly penciled. The nose straight and clean-cut as a Greek statue's. The chin resolute as a boy's. The teeth white and faultless. And the eyes? Well, Peggy Stewart's eyes sometimes made people smile, sometimes almost weep, and invariably brought a puzzled frown to their foreheads. They were the oddest eyes ever seen. Peggy herself often laughed and said:

"My eyes seem to perplex people worse than the elephant perplexed the 'six blind men of Hindustan' who went to SEE him. No two people ever pronounce them the same color, yet each individual is perfectly honest in his belief that they are black, or dark brown, or dark blue, or deep gray, or SEA green. Maybe Nature designed me for a chameleon but changed her mind when she had completed my eyes."

Peggy Stewart would hardly have been called a beautiful girl gauged by conventional standards. Her features were not regular enough for perfection, the mouth perhaps a trifle too large, but she was "mightily pleasin' fer to study 'bout," old Mammy insisted when the other servants were talking about her baby.

"Oh, yes," conceded Martha Harrison, the only white woman besides Peggy herself upon the plantation. "Oh, yes, she's pleasing enough, but if her mother had lived she'd never in this world a-been allowed to run wild as a boy, a-getting tanned as black as a - a, darky."

Martha was a most devoted soul who had come from the North with her mistress when that lady left her New England home to journey to Maryland as Commander Stewart's bride. He was only a junior lieutenant then, but that was nearly eighteen years before this story opens. She had not seen many colored people while living in the Massachusetts town in which she had been born and her experience with them was limited to the very few who, after the Civil War, had drifted into it. Of the true Southern negro, especially those of the ante-bellum type, she had not the faintest conception. It had all been a revelation to her. The devotion of the house servants to their "white folks," to whom so many had remained faithful even after liberation, was a never-ending source of wonder to the good soul. Nor could she understand why those old family retainers stigmatized the younger generations as "shiftless, no-account, new-issue niggers." That there could be marked social distinctions among these colored people never occurred to her.

That generations of them had been carefully trained by master and mistress during the days of slavery, and that the younger generations had had no training whatever, was quite beyond Martha's grasp. Colored people were COLORED PEOPLE, and that ended it.

But as the years passed, Martha learned many things. She had her own neatly-appointed little dining-room in her own well-ordered little wing of the great, rambling colonial house which Peggy Stewart called home, a house which could have told a wonderful history of one hundred eighty or more years. We will tell it later on. We have left Peggy too long perched upon her snake-fence with Shashai and Tzaritza.

The lilting song continued to its end and the dog and horse stood as though hypnotized by the melody and the fingers' magnetic touch. Then the song ended as abruptly as it had begun and Peggy slid lightly from her perch to the ground, raised both arms, stretching hands and fingers and inclining her head in a pose which would have thrilled a teacher of "Esthetic Posing" in some fashionable, faddish school, though it was all unstudied upon the girl's part. Then she cried in a wonderfully modulated voice:

"Oh, the joy, joy, joy of just being ALIVE on such a day as this! Of being out in this wonderful world and free, free, free to go and come and do as we want to, Shashai, Tzaritza! To feel the wind, to breathe it in, to smell all the new growing things, to see that water out yonder and the blue overhead. What is it, Dr. Llewellyn says: 'To thank the Lord for a life so sweet.' WE all do, don't we? *I* can put it into words, or sing it, but you two? Yes, you can make God understand just as well. Let's all thank Him together - you as He has taught you, and I as He has taught me. Now:"

It was a strange picture. The girl standing there in the beautiful early spring world, her only companions a thoroughbred, half-wild Kentucky colt and a Russian wolfhound, literally worth their weight in gold, absolutely faultless in their beauty, and each with their wonderfully intelligent eyes fixed upon her. At the word "Now," the colt raised his perfect head, drew in a deep breath and then exhaled it in a long, trumpet-like whinny. The dog voiced her wonderful bell-like bay; the note of joy sounded by her kind when victory is assured.

The girl raised her head, and parting her lips gave voice to a long-drawn note of ecstasy, ending in a little staccato trill and the same upflinging of the arms.

It was all a rhapsody of springtide, the semi-wild things' expression of intoxicating joy at being alive and their absolute mutual harmony. The animals felt it as the girl did, and surely God acknowledged the homage. Such spontaneous, sincere thanks are rare.

"Let's go now."

The horse's slender flanks quivered; his withers twitched with the nervous energy awaiting an outlet; the dog stood alert for the first motion.

Resting one hand upon those sensitive withers the girl

gave a quick spring, landing lightly as thistledown astride the colt's back, holding the halter strap in her firm, brown fingers. Her costume was admirably adapted to this equestrian if somewhat unusual feat for a young lady. It consisted of a dark blue divided riding skirt of heavy cloth, and a midshipman's jumper, open at the throat, a black regulation neckerchief knotted sailor-fashion on her well-rounded chest. Anything affording freer action could hardly have been designed for her sex. And a bonny thing she looked as she sat there, the soft wind toying with the loose hairs which had escaped their bonds, and bringing the faintest rose tint into her cheeks. It was still too early in the spring for the clear, dark skin to have grown "black as a darky's." "On to the end of nowhere!" she cried. "We'll beat you to the goal, Tzaritza. Go!"

At the word the colt sprang forward with an action so true, so perfect that he and the girl seemed one. The dog gave a low bark like a laugh at the challenge and with incredibly long, graceful leaps circled around and around the pair, now running a little ahead, then executing a wide circle, and again darting forward with that derisive bark.

Shashai's speed was not to be scorned - his ancestors held an international fame for swiftness, endurance and jumping - but no horse can compete with a wolfhound.

On, on they sped, the happiest, maddest, merriest trio imaginable, down the road to the point where the perspective seemed to end it but where in reality it turned abruptly, leaving the one following its course the choice of taking a sudden dip down to the water's edge or wheeling to the right and leaping "brake, bracken and scaur." The girl did not tighten her single guiding strap, she merely bent forward to speak softly into one ear laid back to catch the words:

"Right - turn!"

Just beyond was a high fence dividing the lane where it crossed two estates. It was surmounted by a stile of four steps. There was no pause in the colt's or dog's speed. Tzaritza cleared it like a - wolfhound. Shashai with his rider skimmed over like a bird, landing upon the soft turf beyond with scarcely a sound.

Oh, the beauty of it all! Then on again through a patch of woodland which looked as though a huge gossamer veil had been laid over it. If ever pastelle colors were displayed to perfection Nature here held her exhibition. Soft pinks, pale blues, silver grays, the tenderest greens with here and there a touch of the maple buds' rich mahogany reds, and above and about the maddest melody of bird songs from a hundred throats.

As the horse swung along in his perfect gait, the great dog making playful leaps and feinted snaps at his beautiful muzzle with a dog's derisive smile and sense of humor, and if any one doubts that dogs have this quality they simply don't know the animal, the girl sang at the top of her voice.

They covered the ground with incredible swiftness and presently the lane grew broader, giving evidence of more traffic where a wood road crossed it at right angles. Just a little beyond this point an old gentleman appeared in sight. He was walking with his hands clasped behind him and his head bent to examine every foot of the roadway. Evidently he was too absorbed to be aware of the trio bearing down upon him. He wore the clerical garb of the Church of England, and his face would have attracted attention in any part of the world, it was so pure, so refined, so like a cameo in its delicacy of outline, and the skin held the wonderful softness and clearness we sometimes see in old age. He must have been over seventy.

Just then he became aware of the colt's light hoofbeats and looked up. He was tall and slight but very erect, and his face lighted up with a smile absolutely illuminating as he recognized his approaching friends.

The girl bent forward to say:

"One bell, Shashai." Whereupon her mount slackened his gait to the gentlest amble, but the dog went bounding on to greet the newcomer. First she dropped down at his feet, burying her nose in her forepaws as though to make obeisance, but at his words:

"Ah, Tzaritza! Good Tzaritza, welcome!" she instantly sprang up, rested her forepaws upon his shoulders, and looked into his face with the most limpid pair of eyes ever seen; eyes filled with something deeper than human love can ever summon to human eyes, for those have human speech to supplement their appeal.

"Tzaritza. Dear, faithful Tzaritza," said the old man in the tenderest tone as he caressed the magnificent, silky head now nestling against his face as a child's might have nestled. "Good dog. Good dog. But here are Peggy and Shashai. My little girl, warm greetings," he cried as Shashai came to an instant statue-like standstill at Peggy's one word, "Halt!" and she slid from his back, braced at "attention" and saluted in all gravity, the clergyman returning the salute with much dignity. Then in an instant the martial attitude and air were discarded and springing forward the girl slipped to his side, caught one hand and by a quick, graceful motion circled his arm about her waist and laid her head upon his shoulder just where Tzaritza's had but a moment before rested, her face alight with affection as she exclaimed:

"To meet you 'way, 'way out here, Compadre!"

"'Far from the madding crowd,' Filiola. Five miles to the good for these old legs of seventy-four summers. They have served me well. I have no fault to find with them. They are stanch friends and have carried me many a mile. But you, my child? You and Tzaritza and Shashai? Come hither, my beauty," and the free hand was extended to the colt which instantly advanced for the proffered caress.

"Ah, thou bonny, bonny creature! Thou jewel among thy fellows. Ah, but you possess a masculine frailty. Ah, yes, I've detected it. Oh, Shashai, Shashai, is thy heart reached only through thy stomach?" for now the colt was nozzling most insinuatingly at one of the ample pockets of the old gentleman's top coat. Never had those pockets failed him since the days when he had ceased to be nourished by his dam's milk, and his faith in their bounty was not misplaced, for a slender white hand was inserted to be withdrawn with the lump of sugar Shashai had counted upon and held forth upon the palm from which the velvety lips took it as daintily as a young lady's fingers could have taken it.

Three was the dole evidently for when three had been eaten Shashai gravely bowed his head three times in acknowledgment of his treat and then turned to nibble at the budding trees, his benefactor returning to Peggy.

"So this is heyday and holiday, dear heart, is it? Saturday's emancipation from your old Dominie Exactus when you may range wood and field unmolested, with never a thought for his domination and tyranny."

"As though you ever dominated or tyrannized over me!" protested the girl. "I'd do anything, ANYTHING for you - you know that, don't you?" There was deep reproach in her voice. Then, it changed suddenly as she asked:

"But where is Doctor Claudius?"

"In his stall, eating his fill. I wished to use my own legs today," smiled her companion. "His are exceptionally good ones, but my own will grow stiff if I do not use them more."

Just then Shashai suddenly raised his head and stood with ears alert and nostrils extended. Tzaritza rose from the ground where she had dropped down after greeting Dr. Llewellyn, and stood with ears raised, though neither man nor girl yet heard the faintest sound.

"Some one's coming and coming in a hurry," said Peggy quietly, "or THEY wouldn't look like THAT."

As she spoke the dull thud of hoofs pounding rapidly upon soft turf was borne to their ears, and a moment later a big gray horse ridden by a little negro boy, as tattered a specimen of his race as one might expect to see, came pounding into sight. With some difficulty he brought the big horse to a standstill in front of them and grabbing off his ragged cap stammered out his message:

"Howdy, Massa Dominie. Sarvint, Missy Peggy, but Josh done sont me fer ter fin' yo' an' bring you back yon' mighty quick, kase - kase, de - de sor'el mar' done got mos' kilt an' lak' 'nough daid right dis minit. He say, please ma'am, come quick as Shazee kin fotch yo' fo' de Empress, she mighty bad an' - "

"What has happened to her, Bud?" interrupted Peggy, turning to spring upon Shashai's back, but pausing to learn some particulars. The Empress was one of the most valuable brood mares upon the estate and her foal, still dependent upon her for its nourishment, was Peggy's pride and joy.

"She done got outen de paddock and nigh 'bout bus' herself wide open on de flank on dat dummed MAS-CHINE what dey trims de hedges wid. She bleeged ter bleed ter death, Joshi say."

Peggy turned white. "Excuse me, please - I must go as fast as I can. Home, Shashai, four bells and a jingle!" she cried and the colt swept away like a tornado, Tzaritza in the lead.

"Golly, but she's one breeze, ain' she, sah?"

"She is a wonderful girl and will make a magnificent woman if not spoiled in the next ten years," replied Dr. Llewellyn, though the words were more an oral expression of his own thoughts than a reply to the negro boy.

CHAPTER II

THE EMPRESS

As the half-wild colt swept up to the paddock from which the valuable brood mare Empress had made her escape, Peggy was met by one of the stable hands.

"Where is she?" she asked, her dark eyes full of concern and anxiety.

"Up yonder in de paster," answered the negro, pointing to a green upland. A touch with her heel started Shashai. A moment later she slipped from her mount to hurry to a little group gathered around a dark object lying upon the ground. With the pitiful little cry:

"Oh, Empress! My beauty," Peggy was upon her knees beside the splendid animal.

"Shelby, Shelby, how did it happen? Oh, how did it?" she cried as she lifted the horse's head to her lap. The panting creature looked at her with great appealing, terror-stricken eyes, as though imploring her to save the life-spark now flickering so fitfully.

"God knows, miss," answered the foreman of the paddock. "We did not find her until a half hour ago. If I'd a-found her sooner it would never a-come to this.

We ain't never had no such accident on the estate since *I* been on it, and I'd give all I'm worth if we could a-just have missed THIS one. Some fool, *I* can't find out who, left them hedge shears a-hanging wide open across the gate and the gate unlatched, and she must a run foul of 'em, 'cause we found 'em and all the signs o' what had happened, but we couldn't find HER for more 'n hour, and then THIS is what we found. I sent Bud for you and Jim for the Vet, but we've all come too late." The man spoke low and hurriedly, and never for a moment ceased his care for the mare. The veterinary who had arrived but a few moments before Peggy stood by helpless to do more than had already been done by Shelby, the veteran horse-trainer who had been on the estate for years, and who loved the animals as though they were his children. It was evident that the Empress' moments were numbered. She had severed one of the great veins in her flank and had nearly bled to death before discovered. Her little foal stood near, surprised at his dam's indifference to his needs, his little baby face and great round eyes, so like his mother's, filled with questioning doubt. As Peggy bent over the beautiful dying mare's head, tears streaming from her eyes, for she had cared for her and loved her since colthood, the little foal gave a low nicker and coming up behind the girl, thrust his soft muzzle over her shoulder and nestled his head against her face, trembling and quivering with a terror he could not understand. Peggy raised one arm to clasp it around the little creature's warm neck. The Empress tried to nicker an answer to her baby but the effort cost her last breath and heart-throb. It ended in a fluttering sigh and her head lay still and at rest upon Peggy's lap. The splendid animal, which had so often carried Peggy upon her back, the mother of Shashai, and many another splendid horse whose fame was widely known, lay lifeless. Her little son nestled closer to the one he knew and loved best as though begging her protection. Peggy held him close, sobbing upon his warm neck.

"You'd better get up, Miss Peggy," said Shelby kindly.

Peggy bent and kissed the great silky head. "Good-bye, Empress. I'll care for your baby," she said. Shelby lifted the splendid head from the girl's lap and helped her to her feet. The little colt still huddled close to her.

"Have you any orders, miss, about her?" asked Shelby, nodding toward the dead mare.

"She shall be buried in the circle and shall have a monument. We owe her much. Her foal shall be my charge."

"And I reckon mine, too. If we raise him now it will be a miracle. He's going to miss his dam's milk."

"I think I can manage," answered Peggy. "Bud, come with me. I wish you to go down to Annapolis with a note to Doctor Feldmeyer. He will understand what I wish to do. Ride in on Nancy Lee. Come, little one," and with the little colt's neck beneath her circling arm Peggy walked slowly back to the paddock from which barely three hours before the splendid mare, now lying lifeless in the pasture, had dashed, leaving a trail of her life's blood behind her to guide those who came too late. It was all the outcome of one person's disregard of orders: One of the hands had quit his work to gossip, leaving his great hedge shears hanging carelessly across the gate, and the gate unfastened. The Empress, gamboling with her foal, had rushed upon them, cut herself cruelly, then maddened by the pain and terrified by the flowing blood, had dashed away as only a frightened horse can, running until she fell from exhaustion.

Peggy went back to the inclosure in which the Empress, as the most honored of the brood mares, had lived with her foal. The little stable, a very model of order and appointment, stood at one end of it. She opened the gate, intending to leave the colt in the inclosure, but he huddled closer and closer to her side.

"Why Roy, baby, what is it!" asked Peggy, as she would have spoken to a child. The little thing could only press closer and nicker its baby nicker. Peggy hesitated a moment, then said: "It will never do to leave you now. You are half starved, you poor little thing. Eight weeks are NOT many to have lived. Come." And as though he understood every word and was comforted, the baby horse nickered again and walked close by her side. She went straight to the house, circling the garden, rich in early spring blossoms, to enter a little inclosure around which the servants' quarters were built, one building, a trifle more pretentious than the rest, evidently that of some upper servant. As Peggy and her four-footed companion drew near, a trim little old colored woman looked out of the door. She was immaculate in a black and white checked gingham, a large white apron and a white turban, suggestive of ante-bellum days. Instantly noting signs of distress upon her young mistress' face she hurried toward her, crying softly in her melodious voice:

"Baby! Honey! What's de matter? 'What's done happen? What fo' yo' bring Roy up hyer? Where de Empress at?"

"Oh Mammy, Mammy, the Empress is dead. She - "

"What dat yo' tellin' me, baby? De Empress daid? Ma Lawd, wha' Massa Neil gwine do to we-all when he hyar DAT? He gwine kill SOMEBODY dat's sartin suah. What kill her?"

Peggy told the story briefly, Mammy Lucy, who had been mammy to her and her father before her, listening attentively, nodding her head and clicking her tongue in consternation. Such news was overwhelming.

But Mammy Lucy had not lived on this estate for over sixty years without storing up some wisdom for emergencies, and before Peggy had finished the pitiful tale she was on her way to the great kitchen at the opposite end of the inclosure where Aunt Cynthia ruled as dusky goddess of the shining copper kettles and pans upon the wall.

"Sis Cynthy, we-all in trebbilation and we gotter holp dis hyer pore chile. She lak fer ter breck her heart 'bout de Empress and she sho will if dis hyer colt come ter harm. Please, ma'am, gimme a basin o' fresh, warm milk. Bud he done gone down ter 'Napolis fer a nussin' bottle, but dat baby yonder gwine faint an' die fo' dat no 'count nigger git back wid dat bottle. I knows HIM, I does."

"Howyo' gwine mak' dat colt drink?" asked Cynthia skeptically.

"De Lawd on'y knows, but HE gwine show me how," was Mammy Lucy's pious answer. The next second she cried "Praise Him! *I* got it," and ran into her cabin to return with a piece of snowy white flannel.

Meanwhile Cynthia had warmed the bowlful of milk. Hastily catching up a huge oilcloth apron, Mammy enveloped herself in it and then hurried back to Peggy and her charge.

From that moment Roy's artificial feeding began. Peggy raised his head while Mammy opened his mouth by inserting a skilful finger where later the bit would rest, then slipped in the milk-sopped woolen rag. After a few minutes the small beastie which had never known fear, understood and sucked away vigorously, for he had not fed for hours and the poor inner-colt was grumbling sorely at the long fast. The bowlful of milk soon disappeared, and he stood nozzling at Peggy ready for a frolic, his woes forgotten.

"Now what yo' gwine do wid him, honey?" asked Mammy.

"I'd like to put him to sleep on the piazza, but I'm afraid I can't," answered Peggy, smiling sadly, for the loss of the Empress had struck deeply.

"No, yo' suah cyant do dat," was Mammy's reply. "You'll be bleeged fer ter put him yonder in de paddock."

"He will be so lonesome," said Peggy doubtfully. Just then the great wolfhound came bounding up. She thrust her nose into her mistress' hand and gave a low bark of delight. She was almost as tall as the colt, and seemed to understand his needs. She then turned to give a greeting lick upon the colt's nose. He jerked away, as though resenting the lady's familiarity, but nickered softly. He had known Tzaritza from the first moment he became aware of things terrestrial and they had often gamboled together when the Empress was disinclined for a frolic. Peggy's eyes brightened.

"Tzaritza, attention!"

The splendid hound raised her head to look into her young mistress' eyes with keen intelligence.

"Come," and followed by the hound and colt Peggy hurried back to the stables. They had brought the Empress down from the pasture and laid her upon the soft turf of the large circular grass-plot in front of the main building. The men were now digging her grave.

"Tzaritza, scent," commanded Peggy, stroking the Empress' neck.

The hound made long, deep sniffs at the still form.

"Come." Peggy then laid her hand upon the little colt's neck. The scent was the same. Tzaritza understood.

"Guard," said Peggy.

"Woof-woof," answered Tzaritza deep down in her throat.

Peggy then led the way to the Empress' paddock. Roy capered through the gate; Tzaritza, with her newly-assumed responsibility upon her, entered with dignity. From that hour she scarcely left her charge, lying beside him when he rested in the shade of the great beeches, nestling close in the little stable at night, following him wherever he chose to go during his liberty hours of the day, for thenceforth he was rarely confined to the paddock.

Before the Empress was laid away Bud returned with the nursing bottle. The rubber nipples were thrust into the Empress' mouth and thus getting the mother scent all else was very simple. Roy tugged away at his bottle like a well-conducted, well-conditioned baby, Tzaritza watching with keen intelligent eyes. She soon knew the feeding hours as well as Peggy or Mammy, and promptly to the minute led her charge to Mammy's door. If Mammy happened to be elsewhere she sought Cynthia, and so had the interest grown that there was not a man, woman or child upon the place who would not have dropped anything in order to minister to the needs of Tzaritza's charge.

And so passed the early springtide, Roy waxing fat and strong, Tzaritza never relaxing her care, though at first it was a sore trial to her to remain behind with her foster-son while her beloved mistress galloped away upon Shashai. But that word "Guard" was sacred.

In the course of a few weeks, however, Roy was well able to follow his half-brother, Shashai, and Tzaritza's freedom was restored. The trio was rarely separated and to see Peggy in her hammock on the lawn, or on the piazza, meant to see the colt and Tzaritza also, though Roy was rapidly outgrowing piazzas and lawns, and Peggy was beginning to be puzzled as to what was to be done with him when he could no longer come clattering up the steps and across the piazza after his foster-mother.

With the summer came word that her father would come home on a month's leave and August was longed for with an eagerness he could not have dreamed. Everything must be in perfect order to receive him, and Peggy flew from house to garden, from garden to stables, from stables to paddock keyed to a state of excitement which infected every member of the household. Dr. Llewellyn smiled sympathetically. Harrison, the housekeeper, stalked after her, doing her best to carry out her orders, while announcing that: NOW, she guessed, there would be some hope of making Mr. Neil see the folly of letting a girl of Peggy's age run wild as a hawk forever and a day. She'd have one talk with him he'd do well to take heed to or she'd know why. Mammy Lucy said little but watched her young mistress' radiant face. It was eight months since Master Neil had been home and deep in her tender old heart she understood better than any one else what his coming meant to Peggy. Harrison might have a better idea of what was wise and best for her young charge, but Mammy's love taught her many things which Harrison could never learn.

Meanwhile Peggy spent the greater part of her days down at the paddock, for Shashai must be broken to saddle and bridle in order to receive his master in proper style. A blanket and halter might answer for the mad gallops across country which they had hitherto taken, but Daddy Neil was coming home for a month and the horses must do the place credit.

With this end in view, Peggy betook herself to the paddock one morning before breakfast, saddle and bridle borne behind her by Bud. Shashai welcomed her with his clear nicker, sweeping up to the gate in his long, rocking stride so like the Empress'. Tzaritza with her foster-son followed in Peggy's wake, Tzaritza sniffing inquiringly at the saddle, Roy pranking thither and yonder, rich just in the joy of being alive. Shashai had never quite overcome his jealousy of his young half-brother, and now laid back his ears in reproof of his unseemly gambols; Shashai's own babyhood was not far enough in the background for him to be tolerant.

Peggy entered the paddock and Shashai at once nozzled her for his morning lumps of sugar. For the first time in his memory they were not forthcoming, and his great eyes looked their wondering reproach.

"Not yet, Shashai. "We must keep them for a reward if you behave well." She slipped an arm over the beautifully arched neck and laid her face against the satiny smoothness. Shashai approved the caress but would have approved the sugar much more.

"Give me the saddle, Bud."

The little negro boy handed her the light racing saddle; a very featherweight of a saddle.

"Steady, Shashai."

The colt stood like a statue expecting the girl as usual to spring upon his back. Instead she placed upon it a stiff, leather affair which puzzled him not a little, and from which dangled two curious contrivances. These, however, she quickly caught up and fastened over the back and their metallic clicking ceased to annoy him. The buckling was a little strenuous. Hitherto a surcingle had served to hold the blanket upon his back, but this contraption had TWO surcingles and a stiff leather strap to boot, which Peggy's strong hands pulled tighter than any straps had ever before been pulled around him. He quivered slightly but stood the test and - a lump of sugar was held beneath his eager nostrils, If THAT followed it was worth while standing to have that ugly, stiff thing adjusted.

"Now the headstall, Bud. Did you coat the bit with the melted sugar as I told you?"

"Yes'm, missie. It's fair cracklin' wid sugar, an' onct he gits a lick ob dat bit he ain' never gwine let go, yo' hyar me."

"Now, my bonny one, we'll see," said Peggy, as she unstrapped the bit, and the headstall without it was no more than the halter to which Shashai had been accustomed. Then very gently she held the bit toward him. He tried to take it as he would have taken the sugar and his look of surprise when his lips closed over the hard metal thing was amusing. Nevertheless, it tasted good and he mouthed and licked it, gradually getting it well within his mouth. At an opportune moment Peggy slipped the right buckle into place, quickly following it by the left one. Shashai started.

"Steady, Shashai. Steady, boy," she said gently and the day was won. No shocks, no lashings, no harsh words to make the sight of that headstall throw him into a panic whenever it was produced. Dozens of horses had been so educated by Peggy Stewart. Shashai sucked at his queer mouthpiece as a child would suck a stick of candy, and while he was enjoying its sweetness Peggy brought forth lump number two. Four was his daily allowance, and as he enjoyed number two she let down the stirrups which had seemed likely to startle him.

"Stand outside, Bud, he may be a little frightened when the saddle creaks." The boy left the paddock.

" Stand, Shashai," commanded Peggy, resting her hand

upon the colt's withers. He knew perfectly well what to expect, but why that strange groaning and creaking? The blanket had never done so. The sensitive nerves quivered and he sprang forward, but Peggy had caught her stirrups and her low voice quieted him as she swayed and adapted herself to his gait. Around and around the paddock they loped in perfect harmony of motion. She did not draw upon the bridle rein, merely holding it as she had been accustomed to hold her halter strap, guiding by her knees. Shashai tossed his head partly in nervous irritation at the creaking saddle, partly in the joy of motion, and joy won the day. Then Peggy began to draw slightly upon her reins. The colt shook his head impatiently as though asking: "Wherefor the need? I know exactly where you wish to go."

"Oh, my bonny one, my bonny one, that is just it! I know that you know, but someday someone else won't know, and if I don't teach you now just what the bit means the poor mouth may pay the penalty. It may anyway, in spite of all I can do, but I'll do my best to make it an easy lesson. Oh why, why will people pull and tug as they do on a horse's mouth when there is nothing in this world so sensitive, or that should be so lightly handled. So be patient, Shashai. We only use it because we must, dear. Now, right, turn!" And with the words she pressed her right knee against the colt, at the same time drawing gently upon the right rein. Shashai turned because he had always done so at the words and the pressure, accepting the bit's superfluous hint like the gentleman he was.

"Open the gate, Bud. We'll go for a spin," ordered Peggy as she swung around the paddock.

"Won't yo' jump, missie?" asked Bud eagerly. The delight of his life was to see his young mistress take a fence.

"Not this time," answered Peggy over her shoulder. Bud opened the gate as they came around again and as Peggy cried: "Four bells, Shashai," the colt sprang through, Tzaritza and Roy joining in with a happy bark and neigh.

All so simply, so easily done by love's gentle rule.

CHAPTER III

"DADDY NEIL"

"Stand there, little girl. Why, why - how has it come about! When did you do it? I went away nine months ago leaving a little girl in Mammy Lucy's and Harrison's charge and I have returned to find a young lady. Peggy, baby, what have you done with my little girl?"

Commander Stewart stood in the big living-room of Severndale, his hand upon Peggy's shoulder as he held her at arm's length to look at her in puzzled surprise. He had just experienced one of those startling revelations which often arouse parents to the fact that their children have stolen a march upon them, and sprung into very pleasing young men or women while they themselves have been in an unobserving somnolent state. It is invariably a shock and one which few parents escape.

Peggy laughed, colored a rosy pink but obeyed, a little thrill of innocent triumph passing over her, for Daddy Neil's eyes held something more than surprise, and Peggy's feminine soul detected the underlying pride and admiration.

" By the great god Neptune, you've taken a rise out of

me this time, child. How old ARE you, anyway!"

"As though you didn't know perfectly well, you tease," laughed Peggy, turning swiftly and nestling in his arms. The arms held her closely and the sun-tanned cheek rested upon her dark, silky hair. The eyes were singularly soft and held a suggestion of moisture. It did not seem so very long ago to Daddy Neil since Peggy's beautiful mother had been in that very room with him nestling in his arms in that same confiding little manner. How like her Peggy had grown in looks and a thousand little mannerisms. From the moment Peggy had met him at the Round Bay station to this one, he had lived in a sort of waking dream, partly in the past, partly in the present, and in the strangest possible mental confusion. His memory picture of Peggy as he had left her in October of the previous year was of the little hoyden in short skirts, laughing and prancing from morning till night, and leading Mammy Lucy a life of it.

In nine months the little romp had blossomed into a very charming young girl, dainty and sweet as a wild rose in her white duck sailor suit, with its dark red collar, her hair braided in soft coils about her head and adorned with a big red bow. The embryo woman stood before him.

"Yes, HOW old are you?" he insisted, looking at her with mingled, puzzled eyes.

"Oh, Daddy, you know I was fourteen in January," she said half reproachfully. "You sent me such beautiful things from Japan."

" Yes, but you might be eighteen now from your looks

and height. And living here alone with the servants. Why - why, it's, it's all out of order; you are off your course entirely. You must have someone with you, or go somewhere, or - or - well SOMETHING has got to be done and right off, too," and poor perplexed Neil Stewart ran his hand through his curly, gray-tinged hair in a distracted manner. Peggy looked startled, then serious. Such a contingency as this incumbent upon growing up had never entered her head. Must the old order of things which she so loved, and all the precious freedom of action, give way to something entirely new? Harrison had more than once hinted that such would be the case when Daddy Neil came home and found a young lady where he expected to find a little girl.

"Oh, Daddy, please don't talk about that now. You've only just got here and I've ten thousand things to tell and show you. Let's not think of the future just yet. It's such a joy to just live now. To have you here and see you and hug you, and love you hard," cried Peggy suiting her actions to her words. Mr. Stewart shook his head, but did not beggar his response to the caress. It sent a glow all through him to feel that this beautiful young girl was his daughter, the mistress of the home he so loved, but so rarely enjoyed.

"We'll have a truce for a week, honey, and during that time we'll do nothing but enjoy each other. Then we'll take our reckoning and lay our course by chart, for I'm convinced that I, at least, have been running on dead reckoning and you - well - I guess the good Lord's been at the helm and taken in hand my job with a good deal of credit to Himself and confounded little to me. But it's my watch from now on. I wish your mother were here, sweetheart. You need her now," and Neil

Gabrielle E. Jackson

Stewart again drew the young girl into his strong, circling arm. "I'd resign tomorrow if - if - well, when I resign I want four stripes at least on my sleeve to leave you as a memory in the years to come. Now show me the ropes. I'm a stranger on board my own ship."

For an hour Peggy did the honors of the beautiful home, Jerome, the old butler, who had been "Massa Neil's body servant" before he entered the Academy at eighteen, where body servants had no place, hovering around, solicitous of his master's comfort; Harrison making a hundred and one excuses to come into the room; Mammy Lucy, with the privileges of an old servant making no excuses at all but bobbing in and out whenever she saw fit.

Luncheon was soon served in the wonderful old dining-room, one side of which was entirely of glass giving upon a broad piazza overlooking Round Bay. From this room the view was simply entrancing and Neil Stewart, as he sat at the table at which Peggy was presiding with such grace and dignity, felt that life was certainly worth while when one could look up and encounter a pair of such soft brown eyes regarding him with such love and joy, and see such ripe, red lips part in such carefree, happy smiles.

"Jerome, don't forget Daddy Neil's sauce.

"Yes, missie, lamb. I knows - I knows. Cynthy, she done got it made to de very top-notch pint," answered Jerome, hurrying away upon noiseless feet and in all his immaculate whiteness from the crown of his white woolly head to his duck uniform, for the Severndale servants wore the uniforms of the mess-hall rather than the usual household livery. Neil Stewart could not abide "cit's rigs." Moreover, in spite of the long absences of the master, everything about the place was kept up in ship-shape order; Harrison and Mammy Lucy cooperated with Jerome in looking well to this.

"Now, Daddy," cried Peggy happily when luncheon ended, "come out to the stables and paddock; I've a hundred things to show you."

"A stable and a paddock for an old salt like me," laughed her father. "I wonder if I shall know a horse's hock from his withers? Yet it DOES seem good to see them, and smell the grass and woods and know it's all mine and that YOU are mine," he cried, slipping his arm through hers and pacing off with her. "Some day," he added, "I am coming here to settle down with you to enjoy it all, and when I do I mean to let four legs carry me whenever there is the least excuse for so doing. My own have done enough pacing of the quarter-deck to have earned that indulgence."

"And won't it be just - paradise," cried Peggy rapturously.

They were now nearing the paddock. To one side was a long row of little cottages occupied by the stable hands' families. Mr. Stewart paused and smiled, for out of each popped a funny little black woolly head to catch a glimpse of "Massa Captain," as all the darkies on the place called him.

"Good Lord, where DO they all come from, Peggy? Have they all been born since my last visit? There were not so many here then."

" Not quite all , " answered Peggy laughing. "Most of

them were here before that, though there are some new arrivals either in the course of nature or new help. You see the business is growing, Daddy, and I've had to take on new hands."

Neil Stewart started. "Was this little person who talked in such a matter-of-fact way about "taking on new hands" his little Peggy?

"Yes, yes - I dare say," he answered in a sort of daze.

Peggy seemed unaware of anything the least unusual and continued:

"I want you to see THIS family. It is Joshua Jozadak Jubal Jones'. They might all be of an age, but they are not - quite. Come here, boys, and see Master Captain," called Peggy to the three piccaninnies who were peeping around the corner of the cottage. Three black, grinning little faces, topped by the kinkiest of woolly heads, came slowly at her bidding, each one glancing half-proudly, yet more or less panic-stricken, at the big man in white flannels.

"Hello, boys. Whose sons are you? Miss Peggy tells me you are brothers."

"Yas, sir. We is. We's Joshua Jozadak Jubal Jones's boys. I'se Gus - de ol'es. Der's nine haid o' us, but we's de oniest boys. De yethers ain' nothin' but gurls."

"And how old are you!"

"I'se nine I reckons."

"And what is your name?"

"My name Gus, sah."

"That's only HALF a name. Your whole name is really Augustus remember." The "Massa Captain's" voice boomed with the sound of the sea. Augustus and his brothers were duly impressed. If Gus really meant Augustus, why Augustus he would be henceforth. The Massa Captain had said it and what the Massa Captain said - went, especially when he gave a bright new dime to enforce the order.

"And YOUR name?" continued the questioner, pointing at number two.

"I'se jist Jule, sah," was the shy reply.

"That's a nickname too. I can't have such slipshod, no-account names for my hands' children. It isn't dignified. It isn't respectful. It's a disgrace to Miss Peggy. Do you hear?"

"Yas - yas - sir. We - we hears," answered the little darkies in chorus, the whites of their eyes rolling and their knees fairly smiting together. How could they have been guilty of thus slighting their adored young mistress?

"Please, sah, wha's his name ef taint Jule?" Augustus plucked up heart of grace to ask.

"He is Julius, JUL-I-US, do you understand?"

"Yas - sir. Yas - sir." Another dime helped the memory box.

" And YOUR name ? " asked the Massa Captain of

quaking number three.

There was a long, significant pause, then contortions as though number three were suffering from a violent attack of colic. At length, after two or three futile attempts he blurted out:

"I'se - I'se Billyus, sah!"

There was a terrific explosion, then Neil Stewart tossed the redoubtable Billyus a quarter, crying: "You win," and walked away with Peggy, his laughter now and again borne back to his beneficiaries.

Peggy never knew where that month slipped to with its long rides on Shashai, Daddy Neil riding the Emperor, the magnificent sire of all the small fry upon the place, from those who had already gone, or were about to be sent out into the great world beyond the limits of Severndale, to Roy, the latest arrival. Neil Stewart wondered and marveled more and more as each day slipped by.

Then, too, were the delightful paddles far up the Severn in Peggy's canoe, exploring unsuspected little creeks, with now and again a bag in the wild, lonely reaches of the river, followed by a delicious little supper of broiled birds, done to a turn by Aunt Cynthia. There were, too, moonlight sails in Peggy's little half-rater, which she handled with a master hand. As a rule, one of the boys accompanied her, for the mainsail and centerboard were pretty heavy for her to handle unaided, but with Daddy Neil on board - well, not much was left to be desired. During that month Peggy learned "how lightly falls the foot of time which only treads on flowers," and was appalled when she realized that only five more days remained of her father's leave.

Neil Stewart, upon his part, was sorely perplexed, for it had come to him with an overwhelming force that Peggy was almost a young lady, and to live much longer as she had been living was simply out of the question. Yet how solve the problem? He and Dr. Llewellyn talked long and earnestly upon the subject when Peggy was not near, and fully concurred in their view-point; a change must be made, and made right speedily. Should Peggy be sent to school? If so, where? Much depended upon the choice in her case. Her whole life had been so entirely unlike the average girl's. Why she scarcely knew the meaning of companions of her own age of either sex. Neil Stewart actually groaned aloud as he thought of this.

Dr. Llewellyn suggested a companion for the young girl.

Mr. Stewart groaned again. Whom should he choose? So far as he knew there was not a relative, near or remote, to whom he could turn, and a hit-or-miss choice among strangers appalled him.

"I give you my word, Llewellyn, I'm aground - hard and fast. I can't navigate that little cruiser out yonder," and he nodded toward the lawn where Peggy was giving his first lessons to Roy in submitting to a halter. It was a pretty picture, too, and one deeply imprinted upon Neil Stewart's memory.

"We will do our best for her and leave the rest to the dear Lord," answered the good Doctor, his cameo-like face turned toward the lawn to watch the girl whom he loved as a daughter. "He will show us the way. He has never yet failed to."

"Well, in all reverence, I wish He'd show it before I leave, for I tell you I don't like the idea of going away and leaving that little girl utterly unprotected."

"I should call her very well protected," said Dr. Llewellyn mildly.

"Oh, yes, in a way. You are here off and on, and the servants all the time, but look at the life she leads, man. Not a girl friend. Nothing that other girls have. I tell you it's bad navigating and she'll run afoul rocks or shoals. It isn't natural. For the Lord's sake DO something. If I could be here a month longer I'd start something or burst everything wide open. It's simply got to be changed." And Neil Stewart got up from his big East India chair to pace impatiently up and down the broad piazza, now and again giving an absent-minded kick to a hassock, or picking up a sofa pillow to heave it upon a settee, as though clearing the deck for action. He was deeply perturbed.

Peggy glanced toward him, and quick to notice signs of mental disturbance, left her charge to Tzaritza's care and came running toward the piazza. As she ran up the four steps giving upon the lawn she asked half laughingly, half seriously:

"Heavy weather, Daddy Neil? Barometer falling?"

Neil Stewart paused, looked at her a moment and asked abruptly:

" Peggy, how would you like to go to a boarding school?"

"To boarding school!" exclaimed Peggy in amazement. "Leave Severndale and all this and go away to a SCHOOL?" The emphasis upon the last word held whole volumes.

Her father nodded.

"I think I'd die," she said, dropping upon a settee as though the very suggestion had deprived her of strength.

Her father's forehead puckered into a perplexed frown. If Peggy were sent to boarding school the choice of one would be a nice question.

"Well, what SHALL I do with you?" demanded the poor man in desperation.

"Leave me right where I am. Compadre will see that I'm not quite an ignoramus, Harrison keeps me decently clad and properly lectured, and Mammy looks to my feeding when I'm well and dosing when I'm not, which, thank goodness, isn't often. Why Daddy, I'm so happy. So perfectly happy. Please, please don't spoil it," and Peggy rose to slip her arm within her father's and "pace the deck" as he called it.

"But you haven't a single companion of your own age or station," he protested.

"Do I look the maiden all forlorn as the result?" she asked, laughing up at him.

"You look - you look - exactly like your mother, and to me she was the most beautiful woman I have ever seen," and Peggy found herself in an embrace which threatened to smother her. She blushed with pleasure. To be like her mother whom she scarcely remembered, for eight years had passed since that beautiful mother slipped out of her life, was the highest praise that could have been bestowed upon her.

"Daddy, will you make a truce with me?"

Her father stopped to look down at her, doubtful of falling into a snare, for he had wakened to the fact that his little fourteen-year-old daughter had a pretty long head for her years. Peggy's white teeth gleamed behind her rosy lips and her eyes danced wickedly.

"What are you hatching for your old Dad's undoing, you witch?"

"Nothing but a truce. It is almost the first of September. Will you give me just one more year of this glorious freedom? I shall be nearly sixteen then, and then if you still wish it, I'll go to a finishing school, or any other old school you say to be polished off for society and to do the honors of Severndale properly when you retire. But, Daddy, please, please, don't send me this year. I love it all so dearly - and I'll be good - I truly will."

At the concluding words the big dark eyes filled. Her father bent down to kiss away the unshed tears. His own eyes were troublesome.

"I sign the truce, sweetheart, for one year, but I want a detailed report every week, do you understand?"

"You shall have it, accurate as a ship's log."

Five days later he had joined his ship and Peggy was once more alone, yet, even then, over yonder under the shadow of the dome of the chapel at the Naval Academy the future was being shaped for the young girl: a future so unlike one those who loved her best could possibly have foreseen or planned.

Gabrielle E. Jackson

CHAPTER IV

IN OCTOBER'S DAYS

September slipped by, a lonely month for Peggy as contrasted with August. At first she did not fully realize how lonely, but as the days went by she missed her father's companionship more and more. Formerly, after one of his brief visits she had taken up her usual occupations, fallen back into the old order of things, and been happy in her dumb companions. But this time she could not settle down to anything. She was restless, and as nearly unhappy as it was possible for Peggy Stewart to be. She could not understand it. Poor little Peggy, how could she analyze it? How reason out that her life, dearly as she loved it, was an unnatural one for a young girl, and, consequently, an unsatisfactory one.

Dr. Llewellyn was troubled. Tender, wise and devoted to the girl, he had long foreseen this crisis. It was all very well for the child Peggy to run wild over fields and woodland, to ride, drive, paddle, sail, fish or do as the whim of the moment prompted, happy in her horses and her dogs. Mammy and Harrison were fully capable of looking to her corporal needs and he could look to her mental and spiritual ones, and did do so.

Situated as Severndale was, remote from the other estates upon the river and never brought into social touch with its neighbors, Peggy was hardly known. When Neil Stewart came home on leave he was only too glad to get away from the social side of his life in the service, and the weeks spent with his little girl at Severndale had always been the delight of his life. They took him into a new world all his own in which the small vexations of the outer service world were entirely forgotten.

And how he looked forward to those visits. He rarely spoke of them to his friends, mentioned Severndale to very few and hardly a dozen knew of Peggy's existence. It was a peculiar attitude, but Neil Stewart had never been reconciled to the cruel fate which had taken from him the beautiful wife he had loved so devotedly, and the thought of guests at Severndale without her there to entertain them as she had been accustomed to, was peculiarly abhorent to him. He became almost morbid on the subject and did not realize that he was growing selfish in his sorrow and making Peggy pay the penalty.

But something in the way of an awakening had come to him during his recent visit, and it had shocked him. The child Peggy was a child no longer but a very charming young girl on the borderland of womanhood. In a year or two she would be a young woman and entitled to her place in the social world. Poor Neil Stewart, more than once upon retiring to his bedroom after one of his delightful evenings spent with Peggy, desperately ran his fingers through his curly hair and asked aloud: "What under the sun AM I to do? I can't leave that child vegetating here any longer, yet who will come to live with her or where shall I send her?"

But the question was still unanswered when he left

Severndale and now Peggy was beginning to experience something of her father's unrest.

October came. Her work with Dr. Llewellyn was resumed. Each Sunday she drove into Annapolis to old St. Ann's with Harrison; a modest, unobtrusive little figure who attended the service and slipped away again almost unnoticed. Indeed, if given a thought at all she was vaguely supposed to be some connection of the eminently respectable elderly woman accompanying her. Harrison was a rather stately imposing body in her black taffeta, or black broadcloth, as the season demanded. People did not inquire. It was not their affair. The rector on one or two occasions had spoken to Harrison, but Harrison had been on her dignity. She replied politely but did not encourage intimacy and, if the truth must be confessed, Dr. Smith, rather piqued, decided that he had done his duty and would make no further advances. This had happened some time before the beginning of this story.

In October, as usual, a number of colts were disposed of. Some were sold to people in the adjacent towns or counties, others sent to remote purchasers who had seen them in their baby days, followed their up-bringing and training, and waited patiently for them to arrive at the stipulated age, four years, before becoming their property. No colt was ever sold under four years of age. This was an inviolable law of Severndale, mutually agreed upon by Dr. Llewellyn, the business manager, Shelby, the foreman, and Peggy, the mistress.

"Ain't going to have no half-baked stock sent off THIS place if I have the say-so," had been Shelby's fiat. "I've seen too many fine colts mined by being BRUCK too young and then sold to fools who don't seem to sense that a horse's backbone's like gristle 'fore he's turned three. Then they load him down fit to kill him, or harness him in a way no horse could stand, or drive him off his legs, and, when he's played out, they get back at the man who sold him to them, and like as not there's a lawsuit afoot that the price of the colt four times over couldn't square, to say nothing of a reputation NO stock-farm can afford to have."

Shelby's sense was certainly very sound horse-sense and was rigidly abided by. Consequently, the colts which left Severndale were in the pride and glory of their young horsehood, and this year they were a most promising lot. There were eleven to be disposed of, and, thanks to Peggy's care and training, as fine a bunch of horseflesh as could be found in the land. She had trained - not broken, she could not tolerate that word - every one and each knew his or her name and came at Peggy's call as a child, loving and obeying her implicitly. Among them were two exceptionally beautiful creatures - a splendid chestnut with a white star in the middle of his forehead, and a young filly, half-sister to the chestnut and little Boy. The chestnut was called Silver Star, the filly Columbine, for the singular gentleness of her disposition. She was a golden bay, slender and lithe as a fawn, with great fawn-like brown eyes full of gentleness and love for all, and for Peggy in particular. She had been sold, under the usual conditions during the previous year and was soon to be sent to her new home.

One morning, the second week in October, Peggy opened a letter which held unusual interest for her. It was from a lady whose home was in Wilmot Hall in Annapolis. Wilmot Hall was the hotel near the Naval

Academy and mostly patronized by the officers and their families. The letter was from the wife of a naval officer who wished either to hire or purchase a riding horse for her niece who would spend the winter with her. She stated very explicitly that the horse must be well broken ("Yes, broken!" fairly snorted Peggy. "Broken! I wonder if she would want a literally 'broken' horse? Why will they never say trained!") and gentle, as her niece had ridden very little. The letter then went on to ask if Mrs. Harold might call some day and hour agreed upon. But what amused Peggy most, and caused her to laugh aloud as she took a spoonful of luscious sliced peaches, was the manner in which the letter was addressed.

Old Jerome who was serving her in the pretty delft breakfast-room took an old retainer's privilege to ask:

"What 'musin' you, honey-chile?"

"Didn't know I was an esquire, did you, Jerome? Well I am, because this letter says so. It is addressed to M. C. Stewart, Esq. As I am the only M. C. Stewart I must be the esquire to boot. Wonder what the lady will think when I sign myself Margaret C. Stewart," and Peggy's silvery laugh filled the room.

"Don' yo' mind what dey calls yo', baby. How dey gwine know yo's our young mist'ess? Don' yo' let dat triflin' trebble yo' pretty haid," said the faithful old soul, fearful lest his mistress' pride might be touched, and hastening to serve the second course of her breakfast in his best "quality style."

"It doesn't trouble me even a little bit, Jerome. It's just funny. I'm going to answer that letter right after breakfast, and I wish I could see my correspondent's face when she finds that her 'esquire' is one of her own sex. But I'll never dare let her guess I'm just a girl."

"Jes' a gurl! Jes' a gurl," sputtered Jerome. "Kyant yo' just give her a hint dat yo's a yo'ng lady and we-all's mistiss?"

"'Fraid not, Jerome. She will have to learn that when she comes out here to see Silver Star, if she really comes. I'd let her have Columbine if she were not sold. If that girl, who ever she is, could not ride Columbine she would fall out of a rocking chair. But Star is a darling and never cuts pranks unless Shashai sets him a bad example. I fear Shashai will never forget his colt tricks," and Shashai's mistress wagged her pretty head doubtfully.

"Shas'ee's all right, Miss Peggy. Don' yo' go fer ter 'line him. When I sees yo' two a kitin' way over de fiel's an' de fences, I says ter ma sef, Gawd-a-mighty, Je'ome, yo's got one pintedly hansome yo'ng mistess AN' she kin ride for fair."

"And that same young mistress is in a fair way to be spoiled by your flattery that is pretty certain," laughed Peggy, rising from the breakfast table and gathering up the pile of letters she had been reading.

"Huh, Huh. Spiled nothin'," protested Jerome as she disappeared into the adjoining library.

Seating herself at her very business-like desk she wrote in a clear, angular hand:

Severndale, Round Bay Station.
October 20, 19 -

Mrs. G. F. Harold,
Wilmot Hall,
Annapolis, Md.

Dear Madam:

Your favor of October eighteenth has been duly received and contents noted. In reply would say that I shall be very glad to have you call and inspect our stock.

We have one colt, a four-year old, sired by the Emperor, dam the Empress, which I shall be glad to show you. There are also others, but I am considering pedigree, disposition and gait since you state that you wish a horse for an inexperienced rider.

Would suggest that you run out to Round Bay Station, via B. A. Short Line R. R. on Saturday, October the twenty-third, 1.30 P. M. weather permitting, where I shall meet and convey you to Severndale.

Awaiting your pleasure I am

Very truly yours,

Margaret C. Stewart

How little it often requires to change our whole future. Little did Peggy guess as she wrote that letter in Dr. Llewellyn's most approved form, that it was destined to entirely revolutionize her life, introduce her to a hitherto unknown world and round out her future in a manner beyond the fondest hopes of "Daddy Neil."

This is a big world of little things.

The letter went upon its way and in the course of the morning Peggy almost forgot it.

At ten o'clock Dr. Llewellyn came for the regular morning lessons. If these were a little unusual for a girl of Peggy's age she was certainly none the worse for her very practical knowledge of mathematics, her ability to conduct correctly the business side of the estate, for upon this, as the business manager, good Dr. Llewellyn insisted, and if that bonny, well-poised, level little head sometimes grew weary over investments, and interest, and profits and losses, and nestled down confidingly upon his shoulder, the subjects were none the less fully digested, and Peggy knew to a dollar, as he did, whence her income was derived and to what use it was put.

Then, too, Dr. Llewellyn in his love for the classics made them a fairy world for the girl and the commingling of the practical with the ideal maintained the balance.

When one o'clock came dinner was served and after that Dr. Llewellyn went his way and Peggy hurried off to her beloved horses.

On this day Columbine was to bid good-bye to Severndale. As Peggy entered the big airy stable with its row upon row of scrupulously neat box stalls, for no other sort was permitted in Severndale, Columbine greeted her from one of them, as though asking: "Why am I kept mewed up in here while all my companions are enjoying their daily liberty out yonder?"

Peggy opened the gate and entered the stall. The beautiful creature nestled to her like a petted child.

"Oh, my bonny one, my bonny one, how can I send you away?" asked Peggy softly. "Will they be good to you out yonder? Will they understand what a prize they have got? Washington is far away and so big and so fashionable, they tell me. It would break my heart to have you misused."

The filly nickered softly.

"I am going to send a little message with you. If they read it they will surely pay heed to it."

She drew from the pocket of her blouse a little package. It was not over an inch wide or three long, and was carefully sealed in a piece of oil silk. Parting the thick, luxuriant mane, she tied her missive securely underneath. When the silky hair fell back in place the little message was completely concealed. Peggy clasped her arms about the filly's neck, kissed the soft muzzle and said:

"Good-bye, dear. I'll never forget you and I wonder if I shall ever hear of you or see you again?"

Her eyes were full of tears as she left the stable. Two hours later Columbine was led from her happy home. What later befell her we will learn in a future volume of Peggy Stewart. Meanwhile we must follow Peggy's history.

On the following Saturday, in the golden glow of an

October afternoon, with the hills a glory of color and the air as soft as wine, Peggy drove Comet and Meteor, her splendid carriage horses, to the Bound Bay station to meet Mrs. Harold and her niece. Tzaritza bounded along beside the surrey and old Jess, the coachman of fifty years, sat beside his young mistress, almost bursting with pride as he watched the skill with which she handled the high-spirited animals, for Jess had taught her to drive when she was so tiny that he had to hold her upon his lap, and keep the little hands within the grasp of his big black ones.

Leaving the horses in his care she stepped upon the little platform which did primitive duty as a station, to await the arrival of the electric car which could already be heard humming far away up the line.

As her guests stepped from the car she advanced to meet them, saying as she extended her hand to Mrs. Harold:

"This is Mrs. Harold, I reckon. I am Peggy Stewart. I am glad to meet you."

There was not the least hesitation or self-consciousness and the frank smile which accompanied the words revealed all her pretty, even teeth. "I got your message and I am right glad to welcome you to Severndale."

The lady looked a trifle bewildered. She had expected to meet the owner of Severndale, or, certainly, a mature woman. Her correspondence had, it is true, been with a Margaret C. Stewart, whom she assumed to be Mr. Stewart's wife or some relative. Intuitively Peggy grasped the situation, but kept a perfectly sober face.

"I am very glad to come," said her guest, and added: "This is my niece, Polly Howland."

"It's nice to see and know you. I don't see many girls of my own age. Will you come to the surrey?" and she indicated with a graceful motion of her hand the carriage in waiting just beyond. Mrs. Harold and her niece followed their guide.

Old Jess made a sweeping bow. He must do the honors properly. Peggy helped her guests into the rear seat, then sprang lightly into the front one, drew on a pair of chamois gloves, and taking the reins from Jess, gave a low, clear whistle. Instantly Tzaritza bounded up from beneath some shrubbery where she had lain hidden, and cavorting to the horses' heads made playful snaps at their muzzles. The next second they had reared upon their hind legs. Mrs. Harold gave a little cry of terror and Polly laid hold of the side of the surrey. Peggy flashed an amused, dazzling smile over her shoulder at them as she said reassuringly:

"Don't be frightened. Down, Tzaritza. Steady, my beauties."

At her words the beautiful span settled down as quiet as lambs and swung into a gait which whirled the surrey along the picturesque, woodland road at a rate not to be despised, while Peggy drove with the master-hand of experience. Indeed she seemed to guide more by words than reins, or some perfectly understood signal to the splendid creatures which arched their necks, or laid back an ear to catch each low spoken word.

For a time Peggy's guests were too absorbed in

watching her marvelous skill and almost uncanny power over her horses to make any comment. Then the young girl broke into a perfect ecstasy of delight as she cried:

"Oh, how do you do it? How beautiful they are and what a superb dog. It is a Russian wolfhound, isn't it?"

"Yes, she is a wolfhound. But I don't quite understand. Do what?" and Peggy glanced back questioningly.

"Why drive like that. Make them obey you so perfectly."

"Oh! Why I reckon it is because I have driven all my life. I can't remember when I haven't, and I love and understand them so well. That is all there is to it, I think. They will do almost anything for me. You see I was here when they were born and they have known me from the very first. That makes a lot of difference. And I have a great deal to do about the paddock. I superintend it. The horses are never afraid of me and if they don't know the meaning of fear one can do almost anything with them,"

How simple it was all said. Mrs. Harold was more and more puzzled. The drive was longer than she had expected it to be and she had ample time to observe her young hostess.

"And your mother or aunt, whom I infer is my correspondent, shall I meet her at Severndale!"

"My mother is not living, Mrs. Harold, and I have no own aunt; only an aunt by marriage, the widow of Daddy's only brother, but I have never seen her."

"Then I am at a loss to understand with whom I have been corresponding about a wonderful horse called Silver Star. Someone who signs her letters Margaret C. Stewart, and who evidently knows what she is writing about, too, for she writes to the point and has told me a dozen things which no one but an experienced business woman would think of telling. Yet you tell me there is neither a Mrs. nor Miss Stewart at Severndale."

"I am afraid I am the only Miss Stewart at Severndale, though I am never called Miss Stewart. I'm just Miss Peggy to the help, and Peggy to my friends. But, of course, when I write business letters I have to sign my full name."

"You write business letters. Do you mean to tell me you wrote those letters'?"

"I'm the only Margaret Stewart," answered Peggy, her eyes twinkling. "But here we are at Severndale."

The span made a sharp turn and sped along a beautiful avenue over-arched by golden beeches and a moment later swept up to a stately old colonial mansion which must have looked out over the reaches of Round Bay for many generations.

CHAPTER V

POLLY HOWLAND

It must be admitted that during the drive from the station Peggy's curiosity concerning her guests had been fully as lively as theirs regarding her. She had never known girl friends; there was but one home within reasonable reach of her own which harbored a girl near her own age and during the past year even this one had been sent off to boarding school, her parents realizing that the place was too remote to afford her the advantages her age demanded. Consequently, Peggy experienced a little thrill when she met Polly Howland. Here was a girl of her own age, her own station, and, if intuition meant anything, a kindred spirit. The moment of their introduction had been too brief for Peggy to have a good look at Polly, but now that they had reached Severndale she meant to have it, and while Mrs. Howland and Polly were exclaiming over the beauty of the old place, and the former was wondering how she could have lived in Annapolis so long without even being aware of its existence, Peggy, while apparently occupied in caring for her guests' welfare, was scrutinizing those guests very closely.

What she saw was a lady something past forty, a little above the average height, slight and graceful, with masses of dark brown hair coiled beneath a very pretty

Gabrielle E. Jackson

dark blue velvet toque, a face almost as fresh and fair as a girl's, large, dark brown expressive eyes, which held a light that in some mysterious manner appealed to Peggy and drew her irresistibly. They were smiling eyes with a twinkle suggestive of a sense of humor, a sympathetic understanding of the view-point of those of fewer years, which the mouth beneath corroborated, for the lips held a little curve which often betrayed the inward emotions. Her voice was soft and sweet and its intonation fell soothingly upon Peggy's sensitive ears. Taken altogether, her elder guest had already won Peggy's heart, though she would have found it hard to explain why.

And Polly Howland?

To describe Polly Howland in cold print would be impossible, for Polly was something of a chameleon. What Peggy saw was a young girl not quite as tall as herself, but slightly heavier and straight and lithe as a willow. Her fine head was topped with a great wavy mass of the deepest copper-tinted hair, perfectly wonderful hair, which glinted and flashed with every turn of the girl's head, and rolled back from a broad forehead white and clear as milk. The eyes beneath the forehead were a perfect cadet blue, with long lashes many shades darker than the hair. They were big eyes, expressive and constantly changing with Polly's moods, now flashing, now laughing, again growing dark, deep and tender. The nose had an independent little tilt, but the mouth was exquisitely faultless and mobile and expressive to a rare degree. Polly's eyes and mouth would have attracted attention anywhere.

Of course Peggy did not take quite this analytical view of either of her guests, though in a vague way she felt it all and an odd sense of happiness filled her soul which she would have found it hard to explain.

She led the way through the spacious hall and dining-room to the broad piazza from which the view was simply entrancing, and said:

"Won't you and Miss Howland be seated, Mrs. Harold; I am sure you must be hungry after your ride through this October air. We will have some refreshments and then go out to the paddock to see Silver Star."

Touching a little silver bell, which was promptly answered by Jerome, she ordered:

"Something extra nice for my guests, Jerome, and please send word to Shelby that we will be out to the paddock in half an hour."

"Yes, missie, lamb, I gwine bring yo' a dish fitten f o' a queen."

Mrs. Harold dropped into one of the big East India porch chairs, saying:

"This is one of the most beautiful places I have ever seen. Polly, dear, look at the wonderful reds of those wings contrasted with the foliage back of them. Why have we never known of Severndale? Have you lived here long, Miss Stewart?"

"Would you mind calling me just Peggy? Miss Stewart makes me feel so old and grown-up," said Peggy unaffectedly.

Mrs. Harold smiled approvingly and Polly cried:

"Yes, doesn't it? I hate to be called Miss Howland. I'm not, anyway, for I have an older sister. Have you, too?"

"No," answered Peggy. "I have no one in the world but Daddy Neil, and he is away nearly all the time. I wish he were not. I miss him terribly. He spent August with me and I have never before missed him as I do this time. I have always lived here, Mrs. Harold. I was born here," she concluded in reply to Mrs. Harold's question.

"But your companions?" Mrs. Harold could not refrain from asking.

Peggy smiled.

"That was Daddy Neil's deepest concern during his last visit. He had not thought much about it before, I guess. I dare say you will think it odd, but my companions are mostly four-footed ones, though I am - what shall I call it? Guarded? chaperoned? cared for? by Harrison, Mammy Lucy and Jerome, with my legal guardian, Dr. Llewellyn to keep me within bounds. I dare say most people would consider it very unusual, but I am very happy and never lonely. Yes, Jerome, set the tray here, please," she ended as the butler returned bearing a large silver tray laden with a beautiful silver chocolate service, egg-shell cups straight from Japan, a plate of the most delicate, flaky biscuits, divided, buttered and steaming, flanked by another plate piled high with little scalloped-edged nut cakes, just fresh from Aunt Cynthia's oven.

Taking her seat beside the table Peggy poured and Jerome served in his most dignified manner, while Mrs. Harold marveled more and more and Polly thought she had never in all her life seen a girl quite like Peggy.

"It is one of the most beautiful places I have ever seen," said Mrs. Harold.

"I am glad you like it, for I love it. Few people know of it. I mean few who come to Annapolis. I have lived here so quietly since Mamma's death when I was six years old. Daddy comes whenever he can, but he has asked for sea duty since Mamma left us. He has missed her so."

"In which class did your father graduate, Miss Peggy!"

"In 18 - , Mrs. Harold."

"Why then he must have been in the Academy when Mr. Harold was there. He graduated two years later. I wonder if they knew each other. Mr. Harold would have been a youngster, and your father a first-classman, and first-classmen HAVE been known to notice youngsters."

Peggy looked puzzled. Although she had always lived within ten miles of the Academy, she had never entered its gates, and knew nothing of its ways or rules. Polly was wiser, having spent a month with her aunt. She laughed as she explained:

"A first-classman is a lordly being who is generally at odds with a second-classman, but inclined to protect a third-classman, or youngster, simply because the second-classman is inclined to make life a burden for him, just as he in turn is ready to torment the life out of a fourth-classman, or plebe. I am just beginning to understand it. It seemed perfectly ridiculous at first, but I guess some of those boys are the better for the running they get. I've only been here since the first of October, but I've learned a whole lot in four weeks. Maybe you will come over to see us some time and you will understand better then."

"I'd love to, I am sure. But may I offer you something more? No? Then perhaps we would better go down to the paddock."

They stepped from the piazza and walked through the beautifully kept garden. On either side late autumn flowers were blooming, the box hedges were a deep, waxen green, and gave forth a rich, aromatic odor. Polly cried:

"I just can't believe that you - you - why that you are the mistress of all this. I don't believe you can be one bit older than I am."

"I was fourteen last January," answered Peggy simply.

"And I fifteen last August," cried Polly with the frankness of her years.

"Then you are exactly five months older than I am, aren't you?" Peggy's smile was wonderfully winning.

"And when I look at all this and hear you talk I feel just about five YEARS YOUNGER," was Polly's frank reply. "Why I've never done a single thing in my life."

"Not one?" asked Mrs. Harold, smiling significantly.

"Oh well, nothing like all THIS," protested Polly.

They had now reached a large inclosure. At the further end were a number of low buildings, evidently stables. Nearer at hand, outside the inclosure, were larger buildings - barns and offices. The inclosure was still soft and green in its carpeting of turf and patches of clover. Eight or ten horses were running at large, free and halterless. Further on was another inclosure in which several brood mares were grazing quietly or frisking about with, their colts. Some had come to the high paling to gaze inquiringly at the strangers.

"Oh, Tanta, Tanta, just look at them," cried Polly in a rapture. "And which is to be mine?"

"None of those spindle-legs yonder," was Peggy's amused answer. "They will be running at large for a long time yet. I don't even begin training them until they are a year old - at least not in anything but loving and obeying me. But most of them learn that very quickly. You must look in this paddock for Silver Star, Miss Polly. Shall I call him?"

"Will he really come?" asked Polly incredulously.

For answer Peggy slipped into the paddock, saying as she shot back the bolt:

"We used to have a much simpler fastening, but they learned how to undo it and make their escape. For that reason we are obliged to have these high fences. They have a strain of hunter blood and a six-foot barrier doesn't mean much to some of them."

How bonny the girl looked as she stood there. The horses which were in a little group near the buildings at the opposite end of the paddock, raised their heads inquiringly. The girl gave a long, clear whistle which was instantly answered by a chorus of loud neighs, as the group broke into a mad gallop and bore down upon her. It seemed to Mrs. Harold and Polly as though the on-rushing creatures must bear her down, but just when the speed was the maddest, when heads were tossing most wildly, and tails and manes waving like banners, Peggy cried:

"Halt! Steady, my beauties!" and as one the beautiful animals came to a standstill their hoofs stirring up a cloud of dust, so suddenly did they brace their forefeet. The next second they were crowding around her, nuzzling her hair, her shoulders, her hands, evidently begging in silent eloquence for some expected dainty.

Peggy carried a small linen bag. She opened it and instantly the air was filled with the soft, bubbling whinny with which a horse begs.

"Quiet, Meteor. Be patient, Don. Wait, Queen. Oh, Shashai, will you never learn manners?" she cried as her pet stretched his long neck and catching the little bag in his teeth snatched it from her hands, then, with all the delight of a child who has played a clever trick, away he dashed across the paddock.

"Shashai! Shashai, how dare you! Halt!" she called after him, but the graceful creature had no idea of halting.

For a moment Peggy looked at her guests very much as a baffled schoolmistress might look in the event of her pupil's open defiance, then cried:

" This will never, never do. If he disobeys me once I

shall never be able to do anything with him again. Please excuse me a moment. I must catch him."

"Are you in the habit of chasing whirlwinds?" asked Mrs. Harold laughing.

"You must be able to run faster than most people," laughed Polly, but even as she spoke Peggy cried:

"Star! Star! Come." And out from the group slipped a superb chestnut. He came close to the girl, slipping his beautiful head across her shoulder and nestling against her face with the affection of a child. She clasped her arm up around the satiny neck and said softly:

"We must catch Shashai, Star," then turning like a flash, she rested one hand lightly upon his withers, gave a quick spring and sat astride the horse's back.

Polly gave a little cry and clasped her hands, her eyes sparkling with delight at this marvelous equestrian feat. Mrs. Harold was too amazed to speak.

"After him! Four bells, Star," cried Peggy, and away rushed the pair as though horse and rider were one creature, Peggy's divided cloth skirt, which up to that moment Mrs. Harold had not noticed, fluttering back to reveal the nattiest little patent leather riding boots imaginable. It was one of the prettiest pictures Mrs. Harold and Polly had ever beheld.

But that race was not to end so quickly. Shashai boasted the same blood as Silver Star, and was every bit as intelligent as his older brother. Moreover he had no mind to give up his treasure-trove. He knew that little bag and its contents too well and was minded to carry it to the end of the paddock and there rend and tear it, until its contents were spilled and he could eat his companions' share as well as his own. And that was exactly what Peggy did not propose to permit, either for his well-being or in justice to the other pets.

As the extraordinary game of tag ranged around the big paddock, Polly fairly danced up and down in excitement, crying:

"Tanta, Tanta, I didn't know any one COULD ride like that girl. Why it is more wonderful than a circus. And isn't she beautiful? Oh, I want to know her better. I am sure she must be a perfect dear. Why if I could ever ride half as well I'd be the proudest girl in the world."

"And how simply and unostentatiously she does everything. Polly, I suspect we shall be the richer for several things besides a handsome horse when we return to Wilmot."

Meanwhile Peggy was bearing down upon the thief and his plunder, though he darted and dodged like a cat, but in an unguarded moment he gave Star the advantage and was cornered.

"Shashai, halt! Steady. Down. My pardon."

Never was human speech more perfectly understood and obeyed. The game was up and the superb horse stopped, dropped upon his knees and touched the ground with his muzzle, the bag still held in his teeth.

"Up, Shashai," and the horse was again upon his feet.

Peggy reached over and taking hold of his flowing

forelock led him back to the gate. Nothing could have been more demure than the manner in which he minced along beside her. At the gate Peggy slipped from Star's back as snow slips from a sunny bank, and stretching forth her hand said:

"Give it to me, Shashai."

The mischievous colt dropped the bag into her hand.

"Good boy," and a caress rewarded the reformed one.

Then Polly's enthusiasm broke forth.

How had she ever done it? Who had taught her to ride like that? Could she, Polly, ever hope to do so?

Peggy laughed gaily, and explained Shelby's methods as best she could, giving a little outline of her life on the estate which held a peculiar interest for Mrs. Harold, who read more between the lines than Peggy guessed, and who then and there resolved to know something more of this unusual girl to whose home they had been so curiously led. She had been thrown with young people all her life and loved them dearly, and here to her experienced eyes was a rare specimen of young girlhood and her heart warmed to her.

"I'd give anything to ride as you do," said Polly quite in despair of ever doing so.

"Why I can't remember when I haven't ridden. Shelby put me on a horse when Mammy Lucy declared I was too tiny to sit in a chair, and oh, how I love it and them. It is all so easy, so free - so - I don't quite know how to express it. But I must not take any more of your time talking about myself. Please excuse me for having talked so much. I wanted you to see Silver Star's paces but I did not plan to show them in just this way. But isn't he a dear? I don't know how I can let him go away from Severndale, but he as well as the others must. We sent Columbine only a few days ago. She has the sweetest disposition of any horse I have ever trained. It nearly broke my heart to send her off. They are all relatives. Shashai and Star are half-brothers. Shashai is my very own and I shall never sell him. Would you like to try Star, Miss Polly? I can get you a riding skirt. Shall you ride cross or side? He is trained for both."

"Not today, I think," answered Mrs. Harold for Polly. "We must make our arrangements for Star and then we will see about riding lessons. I wish you would undertake to teach Polly."

"Oh, would you really let me teach her?" cried Peggy enthusiastically.

"I think the obligation would be all on the other side," laughed Mrs. Harold. "It would be a privilege too great to claim."

"There would be no obligation whatever. I'd just love to," cried Peggy eagerly. "Why it would be perfectly lovely to have her come out here every day. Please walk back to the house and let us talk it over," Peggy's eyes were sparkling.

"Oh, Tanta, may I?"

"Slowly, Polly. My head is beginning to swim with so many ideas crowding into it," but Polly Howland knew from the tone that the day was as good as won.

CHAPTER VI

A FRIENDSHIP BEGINS

As they walked back to the house the girls talked incessantly, Mrs. Harold listening intently but saying very little. She was drawing her own conclusions, which were usually pretty shrewd ones.

Commander Harold had for the past four years been stationed either at the Naval Academy, or on sea duty on board the Rhode Island when she made her famous cruise around the world. Mrs. Harold had remained at Wilmot Hall during the winter of 1907 and 1908, Polly's sister Constance spending it with her. Later Commander Harold had duty at the Academy, but recently with his new commission, for he had been a commander only a few months, he had been given one of the new cruisers and was at sea once more. They had no children, their only child having died many years before, but Mrs. Harold, loving young people as she did, was never without them near her. This winter her niece, Polly Howland, would remain with her and she was anxious to make the winter a happy one for the young girl. This she had a rare opportunity of doing, for her pretty sitting-room in Wilmot Hall was a gathering place for the young people of the entire neighborhood and the midshipmen in particular, who loved it dearly and were devoted to its mistress, loving her with the devotion of sons, and invariably calling her "the Little Mother," and her sitting-room "Middies' Haven." And a happier little rendezvous it would have been hard to find, for Mrs. Harold loved her big foster-sons dearly, strove in every way to make the place a home for them and to develop all that was best in their diverse characters.

It was to this home that Polly had come to pass the winter and now a new phase had developed, the outcome of what seemed to be chance, but it is to be questioned whether anything in this great world of ours is the outcome of chance. If so wisely ordered in some respects, why not in all?

So it is not surprising that Mrs. Harold watched and listened with rare sympathy and a keen intuition as the girls walked a little ahead of her, talking together as freely and frankly as though they had known each other for years instead of hours only.

"Couldn't you come out on the electric car every morning?" Peggy was asking. "If you could do that for about two weeks I am sure you would be able to ride BEAUTIFULLY at the end of them."

"Not in the morning, I'm afraid. You see I am an Annapolis co-ed," Polly answered laughing gaily at Peggy's mystified expression. "Yes I am, truly. You see I came down here to spend the winter with Aunt Janet because she is lonely when Uncle Glenn is away. But, of course, I can't just sit around and do nothing, or frolic all the time. Had I remained at home I should have been in my last year at high school, but Tanta doesn't want me to go to the one down here. Oh we've had the funniest discussions. First she thought she'd engage a governess for me, and we had almost settled on that when the funniest little thing changed it all. Isn't it queer how just a little thing will sometimes turn your plans all around?"

"What changed yours?" asked Peggy, more deeply interested in this new acquaintance and the new world she was introducing her into than she had ever been in anything in her life. "You'll laugh at me, I dare say, if I tell you, but I don't mind. Up at my own home in Montgentian, N. J., I had a boy chum. We have known each other since we were little tots and always played together. He is two years older than I am, but I was only a year behind him when he graduated from the high last spring. My goodness, how I worked to catch up, for I was ashamed to let him be so far ahead of me. I couldn't quite catch up, though, and he graduated a year ahead of me in spite of all I could do. Then he took a competitive examination for Annapolis and passed finely, entering the Academy last June. I was just tickled to death for we are just like brother and sister, we have been together so much. Then Tanta sent for me and I came back with her on September 30. One day we were over in the yard and the boys - men, I dare say I ought to call them, for some of them are tall as bean poles, only they have all been Aunt Janet's 'boys' ever since they entered the Academy - were teasing me, and telling me I couldn't work with Ralph any longer. I got mad then and said I guessed I COULD work with him if I saw fit, and I meant to, too. Oh, they laughed and jeered at me until I could have slapped every single one of them, but I then and there made up my mind to follow THIS year's academic course if I died in the attempt, and when we went home I talked it all over with Aunt Janet. She's such a dear, and always ready to listen to anything we young people have to tell her. So I really am a co-ed. Yes, I am; I knew you'd smile. I have an instructor, a retired captain, a friend of Aunt Janet's, who lives at Wilmot, and Aunt Janet has rented an extra room next mine for a schoolroom, and every morning at nine o'clock Captain Pennell and I settle down to real hard work. I have 'math' and mechanical drawing just exactly as Ralph has, and the same French, Spanish and English course, but what I love best of all is learning all about a boat and how to sail her, how to swim, and the gym work. And Captain Pennell is teaching me how to fence and to shoot with a rifle and a revolver. Oh, it is just heaps and heaps of fun. I didn't dream a girl could learn all those things, but Captain Pennell is such a dear and so interesting. He seems to have something new for each day. But HOW Aunt Janet's boys do run me and ask me when I'm coming out for cutter drill, or field artillery or any old thing they know I CAN'T do. But never mind. I know just exactly what all their old orders mean, and I am learning all about our splendid big ships and the guns and everything just as fast as ever I can. But, my goodness, I shall talk you to death. Mother says I never know when to stop once I get started. I beg your pardon," and Polly looked quite abashed as they drew near the piazza.

"Why I think it is all perfectly fascinating. How I'd love to do some of those things. I can shoot and swim and sail my boat, but I've never been in a gymnasium or done any of those interesting things. I wish Compadre could hear all about it. They wanted to send me away to a big finishing school this winter but I begged so hard for one more year's freedom that Daddy Neil consented, but I think he would love to have me know about the things you are learning."

"Oh, Tanta, couldn't we make some sort of a bargain? Couldn't Peggy come to us three days of the week and work with Captain Pennell and me, and then I come out three to learn to ride?"

Peggy's eyes shone as she listened. She had not realized how hungry she had been for young companionship until this sunny-souled young girl had dropped into her little world.

Mrs. Harold smiled sympathetically upon the enthusiastic pair.

"Perhaps we can make a mutually beneficial bargain," she said. "I think I shall accept Silver Star upon your recommendation, Miss Peggy, and what I have already seen. Then if you are willing to undertake it, Polly shall be taught to ride by you, and you in turn must come to us at Wilmot to join Captain Pennell's class of fencing, gym work or whatever else seems wise or you wish to. But who must decide the question, dear?"

How unconsciously she had dropped into the term of endearment with this young girl. It was so much a part of her nature to do so. Peggy's cheeks became rose-tinted with pleasure, and her eyes alight with happiness. Her smile was radiant as she slipped to Mrs. Harold's side saying: "Oh, if Compadre were only here to decide it right away. He is my guardian you know, and, of course, I must do as he wishes, but I hope - oh I HOPE, he will let me do this."

"And what is it you so wish to do, Filiola?" asked a gentle voice within the room.

Peggy gave a little cry of delight.

"Oh, Compadre, when did you come? We have just been talking about you," cried Peggy, flitting to the side of the tall, handsome old gentleman and slipping her arm about him as his encircled her shoulder, and he looked down upon her with a pair of benign dark eyes as he answered:

"I have been luxuriating and feasting for the past half hour while waiting for a truant ward. Jerome took pity upon me and fed me to keep me in a good temper.

"Oh, Compadre, I want you to know my new friend, Mrs. Harold and her niece, Polly Howland. We have been having the loveliest visit together."

Dr. Llewellyn advanced to meet the guests, one arm still encircling his ward, the other extended to take Mrs. Harold's hand as he said:

"This is a great pleasure, madam. To judge by my little girl's face she has found a congenial companion. I am more than delighted to meet both aunt and niece."

"And we are ALMOST the same age! Isn't that lovely!" cried Polly.

Dr. Llewellyn exchanged a significant glance with Mrs. Harold, then asked:

"Have you imparted your peculiar power to your niece, Mrs. Harold?"

Mrs. Harold looked mystified. "I am afraid I don't quite understand," she smiled.

" Your chaplain at the Academy is an old friend of

mine. We occasionally hobnob over the chess board and a modest glass of wine. I hear of things beyond Round Bay and Severndale; I am interested in that gathering of young men in the Academy and often ask questions. The chaplain is deeply concerned for their welfare and has told me many things, among others something of a certain lady to whom they are devoted and who has a remarkable influence over them. It has interested me, too, for they are at the most impressionable, susceptible period of their lives and a wise influence can do much for them. I am glad to meet 'The Little Mother of Middies' Haven.'"

Dr. Llewellyn's eyes twinkled as he spoke. Mrs. Harold blushed like a girl as she asked:

"Have my sins found me out?"

"It is a pity we could not find all 'sins' as salutary. I may be a retired old clergyman, with no greater responsibilities upon my shoulders than keeping one unruly little girl within bounds," he added, giving a tweak to Peggy's curls, "and looking after her father's estate - I tutored HIM when he was a lad - but I hear echoes of the doings of the outer world now and again. Yes - yes, now and again, and when they are cheering echoes I rejoice greatly. But let us be seated and hear the wonderful news which will cause an explosion presently unless the safety-valves are opened," he concluded, placing chairs for Mrs. Harold and Polly with courtly grace.

They talked for an hour and at its end Dr. Llewellyn and Mrs. Harold had settled upon a plan which caused Peggy and Polly to nearly prance for joy.

Mrs. Harold was to talk it over with Captain Pennell and phone out to Severndale the next morning, and if all went well, Peggy would go to Annapolis to take up certain branches of the work with Polly, and in the intervening mornings continue her work with Dr. Llewellyn, and Polly in return would spend three afternoons with her.

Star was hired then and there for the winter, but would live at Severndale until Polly's horse-WOMAN-ship was a little more to be relied upon.

Before Mrs. Harold and Polly realized where the afternoon had gone it was time to return to Annapolis. They were driven to the station by Jess, Peggy and Dr. Llewellyn riding beside the carriage on Shashai and Dr. Claudius, Dr. Llewellyn's big dapple-gray hunter, for the old clergyman was an aristocrat to his fingertips and lived the life of his Maryland forebears, at seventy sitting his horse as he had done in early manhood, and even occasionally following the hounds. It was a pretty sight to see him and Peggy ride, his great horse making its powerful strides, while Shashai flitted along like a swallow, full of all manner of little conceits and pranks though absolutely obedient to Peggy's low-spoken words, or knee-pressure, for the bridle rein was a quite superfluous adjunct to her riding gear, and she would have ridden without a saddle but for conventionalities.

They bade their guests good-bye at the little station, and rode slowly back to Severndale in the golden glow of the late afternoon, Peggy talking incessantly and the good doctor occasionally asking a question or telling her something of the world over in the Academy of which she knew so little, but of which fate seemed to have ordained she should soon know much more.

There was a quiet little talk up in Middies' Haven that evening, and Captain Pennell learned from Mrs. Harold of the little girl up at Round Bay. He was not only willing to accept Peggy as a second pupil, but delighted to welcome the addition to his "Co-ed Institution" as he called it. He had grown very fond of his pupil in the brief time she had worked with him, but felt sure that a little competition would lend zest to the work. He was deeply interested in the novel plan and wished his pupil to give her old chum and schoolmate a lively contest. Moreover, he was a lonely man whom ill-health and sorrow had left little to expect from life. His wife and only daughter had died in Guam soon after the end of the Spanish war, in which he had received the wound which had incapacitated him for service and forced him to retire in what should have been the prime of life. Since that hour he had lived only to kill time; the deadliest fate to which a human being can be condemned. Until Polly entered his lonely world it would have been hard to picture a duller life than he led, but her sunshiny soul seemed to have reflected some of its light upon him, and he was happier than he had been in years.

It is safe to say that the description of Peggy, her home, her horses and all pertaining to her, lost nothing in Polly's telling and it was agreed that she should become a special course co-ed upon the following Monday.

And out at Severndale an equally eager, enthusiastic little body was awaiting the ringing of the telephone bell, and when at nine o'clock Sunday morning its cheerful jingling summoned Peggy from her breakfast table, she was as happy as she well could be and promised faithfully to be at Wilmot at nine o'clock the following morning.

And so began a friendship destined to last as long as the girls lived, and the glorious autumn days were filled with delights for them both. To Peggy it was a wonderful world.

The Tuesday following Polly went to Severndale and her first riding lesson began, with more or less quaking upon her part, it must be confessed. She felt tremendously high up in the air when she first found herself upon Silver Star's back. But he behaved like a gentleman, seeming to realize that the usual order of things was being reversed and that he was teaching instead of being taught. So, in spite of Shashai's wicked hints for a prank, he conducted himself in a manner most exemplary and Polly went back to Wilmot Hall as enthusiastic as she well could be.

Mrs. Harold had invited Peggy to spend the week-end at Wilmot. She wished her to meet some of Polly's friends and she, herself, wished to know the young girl better. So Dr. Llewellyn's permission was asked and promptly granted, and with his consent won that of Harrison and Mammy Lucy was a mere form. Nevertheless, Peggy was too wise to overlook asking, for Harrison fancied herself the embodiment of the law, and Mammy Lucy, in her own estimation at least, stood for the dignity of the Stewart family. And the preparations for the little week-end visit were undertaken with a degree of ceremony which might have warranted a trip to Europe. Peggy's suitcase was packed by Mammy's own hands, Harrison hovering near to make sure that nothing was overlooked, to Mammy's secret disgust, for she felt herself fully capable of attending to it.

Then came the question of going in, Peggy very naturally expecting to go by the electric car as she had during the week. But NO! Such an undignified entrance into Wilmot was not to be thought of. She must be driven in by Jess.

"But Mammy, how ridiculous," protested Peggy. "I can get a boy at the station to carry my suitcase to the hotel."

Mammy looked at her in disdain.

"Git one ob dem no 'count dirty little nigger boys what hangs round dat railway station to tote yo' shute case, a-tailin' long behime yo' for all de worl lak a tromp. What yo' 'spose yo' pa would say to we-all if we let yo' go a-visitin' in amy sich style as dat, an' yo' a Stewart AN' de daughter ob a naval officer who's gwine visit de wife ob one ob his 'Cademy frien's! Chile, yo's cl'ar crazy. Yo' go in de proper style lemme tell yo', or yo' aim gwine go 'tall. Yo' hear ME?"

And Peggy had to meekly submit, realizing that there were SOME laws which even a Stewart might not violate. So on Saturday afternoon Comet and Meteor tooled the surrey along by beautiful woodland and field, Peggy clad in her pretty autumn suit and hat, her suitcase at Jess' feet, and herself as properly dignified as the occasion demanded, while in her secret heart she resolved to enlist Mrs. Harold upon her side and in future make her visits with less ceremony.

CHAPTER VII

PEGGY STEWART: CHATELAINE

Peggy had entered a new world. Plunged into one, would perhaps better express it, so sudden had been her entrance, and her letters to Daddy Neil, now on his way to Guantanamo for the fall drills, were full of an enthusiasm which almost bewildered him and started a new train of thought.

As he knew most members of the personnel of the ships comprising the Atlantic fleet, he, of course, knew Commander Harold, though it had never occurred to him to associate him with Annapolis, or to make any inquiry regarding his home or his connections. Like many another, he was merely a fellow-officer. He was not a classmate, so his interest was less keen than it would have been had such been the case. Moreover, Harold was in a different division of the fleet and they very rarely met. But now the whole situation was changed by Peggy's letter. He would hunt up Mr. Harold at the first opportunity and with this common interest to bind them, much pleasure was in store.

True to her word, Peggy sent her letter off every Sunday afternoon - a conscientious report of the week's happenings. Her "log," she called it, and it was the comfort of Daddy Neil's life.

Meanwhile, she spent about half of her time with Mrs. Harold and Polly, and in a very short time became as good a chum of Mrs. Harold's "boys," the midshipmen, as was Polly. There was always something doing over at the Academy, and as Mrs. Harold's guest, Peggy was naturally included. At present football practice was absorbing the interest of the Academic world and its friends, for in a few weeks the big Army-Navy game would take place up in Philadelphia and Mrs. Harold had already invited Peggy to go to it with her party. Peggy had never even seen a practice game until taken over to the Naval Academy field with her friends, where the boys teased her unmercifully because she asked why they didn't "have a decently shaped ROUND ball instead of a leather watermelon which wouldn't do a thing but flop every which way, and call it tussle-ball instead of football?"

There was a little circle which gathered about Mrs. Harold, and which was always alluded to as "her big children." These were men from the different classes in the Academy, for there were no "class rates" in "Middies' Haven," as they called her sitting-room. Peggy met them all, though, naturally, there were some she liked better than others. Among the upper-classmen who would graduate in the spring were three who were at Middies' Haven whenever there was the slightest excuse for being there. These boys who seemed quite grown-up men to fourteen-year-old Peggy, though she soon lost her shyness with them, and learned that they could frolic as well as the younger ones, went by the names of Happy, Wheedles and Shortie, the latter so nicknamed because he was six feet, four inches tall, though the others' nicknames had been bestowed because they really fitted. There were also two or three second-classmen and youngsters who frequently visited Mrs. Harold, one in particular, who fascinated every one with whom he came in touch. His name was Durand Leroux, and, strange to state, he looked enough like Peggy to be her own brother, yet try as they would, no vestige of a relationship could be traced, for Peggy came of purely Southern stock while Durand claimed New England for his birthplace. Nevertheless, it became a good joke and they were often spoken of as the twins, though Durand was three years Peggy's senior.

Polly's chum, Ralph Wilbur, was about the same age as Durand, though in the lowest or fourth class, having just entered the Academy, and consequently was counted as very small fry indeed. He was a quiet, undemonstrative chap but Peggy liked him from the moment she met him. He had mastered one important bit of knowledge: That a "plebe" does well to lie low, and as the result of mastering that salient fact he was well liked by the upper-classmen and found them ready to do him a good many friendly turns which a more "raty" fourth-classman would not have found coming his way.

Altogether, Peggy found herself a member of a very delightful little circle and was happier than she had ever been in her life. In Mrs. Harold she found the love she had missed without understanding it, and in Polly a companion who filled her days with delight.

And what busy days they were. So full of plans, duties and pleasures, for Mrs. Harold had been very quick to understand the barrenness of Peggy's life in spite of her rich supply of this world's goods, and she promptly set about rounding it out as it should have been.

And so November with its wonderful Indian Summer slipped on, and it was during one of these ideal days that an absurd episode took place upon the well-conducted estate of Severndale, which caused Peggy to be run most unmercifully by the boys. But before we can tell of it a few words of explanation are needed.

As can be readily understood, in a large institution like the Naval Academy, where the boys foregather from every state in the Union, there are all classes and all types represented.

Among them are splendid, fine principled fellows, with high moral standards and unimpeachable characters. And there are, alas, those of another type also, and these are the ones who invariably make trouble for others and are pretty sure to disgrace themselves. Fortunately, this type rarely survives the four years' crucial test of character, efficiency and aptitude, but is pretty sure to "pack its little grip and fade away," as the more eligible ones express it, long before it comes time to receive a diploma.

Unhappily, there was one man in the present first class who had managed to remain in the Academy in spite of conduct which would have "bilged" (Academy slang for the man who has to drop out) a dozen others, and who was the source of endless trouble for under-classmen over whom he contrived to exert a wholly malign influence. He seemed to be not only utterly devoid of principle and finer feeling, but to take a perfectly fiendish delight in corrupting the younger boys. His one idea of being "a man" seemed to lie in the infringement of every regulation of the Academy, and to induce others to do likewise. He had caused the president of his class endless trouble and mortification, and distressed Mrs. Harold beyond measure, for her interest in all in the Academy was very keen, and especially in the younger boys, whom she knew to be at the most susceptible period of their lives.

Had his folly been confined to mere boyish nonsense it might have been overlooked, but it had gone on from folly to vicious conduct and his boast was that it was his duty to harden the plebes, his idea of hardening them being to get them intoxicated.

Now if there is one infringement of rules more sure to bring retribution upon the perpetrator than any other, it is intoxication, and the guilty one is most summarily dealt with. This was fully known to Blue, the delinquent referred to, but he had by some miraculous method thus far managed to escape conviction if not suspicion, though more than one unfortunate under-classman had been forced to tender his resignation as the result of going the pace with Blue.

So serious had the situation become that the president of the first class had quietly set about a little plan in cooperation with other members of his class which would be pretty sure to rid the Academy of its undesirable acquisition. It was only a question of giving Blue enough time to work his own undoing, and as things had begun to shape, this seemed pretty sure to take place. Naturally, with feeling running so strong, Peggy heard a good deal of it when she visited Middies' Haven, especially since Durand Leroux, whom she had grown to like so well, seemed to have been selected by Blue as his newest victim, greatly to Mrs. Harold's distress, for she knew Durand to be far too easily led, and too generous and unsuspicious to believe evil of any one. Happy-go-lucky, carefree and ever ready for any frolic, he was exactly the type to fall a victim to Blue's insidious influence, for Blue could be fascinating to a degree when it served his turn. Blue was debarred the privilege of visiting Middies' Haven, and his resentment of this prompted him to try to wreak his vengeance upon Mrs. Harold's boys. To their credit be it told that he had hitherto failed, but she had misgivings of Durand; he was too mercurial.

Now Peggy had, as chatelaine of Severndale, been more than once obliged to order the dismissal of some of the temporary hands employed about the paddock, for Shelby was rigid upon the rule of temperance. He would have no bibblers near the animals under his charge. He had seen too much trouble caused by such worthless employees. Consequently, Peggy was wise beyond her years to the gravity of intemperance and had expressed herself pretty emphatically when Blue was discussed within the privacy of Middies' Haven, for what was told there was sacred. That was an unwritten law. And all this led to a ridiculous situation one day in the middle of November, for comedy and tragedy usually travel side by side in this world.

It fell upon an ideal Saturday afternoon, a half-holiday at the Academy. It also happened to be Wheedles' birthday, and Mrs. Harold never let a birthday pass without some sort of a celebration if it were possible to have one. She had told Peggy about it, and Peggy had promptly invited a little party up to Round Bay.

Now visiting for the midshipmen beyond the confines of the town of Annapolis is forbidden, but Mrs. Harold, as the wife of an officer, was at liberty to take out a party of friends in one of the Academy launches, so she promptly got together a congenial dozen, Ralph,

Gabrielle E. Jackson

Happy, Shortie, Wheedles and Durand, Captain Pennell and four others besides Polly and herself, and in the crispness of the Indian Summer afternoon, steamed away up the Severn to Round Bay.

Peggy had asked the privilege of providing the birthday feast and understanding the pleasure it would give her to do so, Mrs. Harold had agreed most readily. So immediately after luncheon formation the party embarked at the foot of Maryland Avenue and a gayer one it would have been hard to find.

Knowing the average boy's appetite and the midshipman's in particular, Mrs. Harold had, with commendable forethought, brought with her a big box of crullers, in nowise disturbed by the thought that it might spoil their appetites for the delayed luncheon. Breakfast is served at seven A.M. in Bancroft Hall, and the interval between that and twelve-thirty luncheon is long enough at best. If you add to that another hour and a half it is safe to conclude that starvation will be imminent. Hence her box of crullers to avoid such a calamity.

The launch puffed and chugged its way up the river, running alongside the pretty Severndale dock sharp to the minute of four bells. Peggy stood ready to welcome them.

"Oh, isn't this lovely. Scramble ashore as fast as you can, for Aunt Cynthia is crazy lest her fried chicken 'frazzle ter a cinder,'" she cried as she greeted her guests.

"Who said fried chicken?" cried Happy.

"That last cruller you warned me against eating never fazed me a bit, Little Mother," asserted Wheedles, as he assisted Mrs. Harold up the stone steps leading from the dock.

"Beat you in a race to the lawn, Polly," shouted Ralph, back in boyhood's world now that he was beyond the bounds of Bancroft, and the next moment he and Polly were racing across the lawn like a pair of children, for it seemed so good to be away for a time from the unrelaxing discipline of the Academy, and Polly realized this as well as the others.

"We are to have luncheon out under the oaks," said Peggy. "It is too heavenly a day to be indoors. Jerome and Mammy have everything ready so we have nothing to do but eat. You won't mind picnicking will you, Mrs. Harold."

"Mind!" echoed Mrs. Harold. "Why it is simply ideal, Peggy dear. What do you say, sons?" she asked turning to the others.

"Say! Say! Let's give the Four-N Yell right off for Peggy Stewart, Chatelaine of Severndale!" cried Wheedles, and out upon the clear, crisp autumn air rang the good old Navy cheer:

"N - n - n - n!
A - a - a - a!
V - v - v - v!
Y - y - y - y!

Navy!

Gabrielle E. Jackson

Peggy Stewart! Peggy Stewart!
Peggy Stewart!"

Peggy's cheeks glowed and her eyes shone. It was something to win that cheer from these lads, boys at heart, though just at manhood's morning, and sworn to the service of their flag. How she wished Daddy Neil could hear it. Captain Pennell, into whose life during the past month had come some incentive to live, joined in the yell with a will, giving his cap a toss into the air when the echoes of it went floating out over the Severn, while Mrs. Harold and Polly waved their sweaters wildly, and yelled with all their strength.

Never had Severndale been more beautiful than upon that November afternoon. October's rich coloring had given place to the dull reds, burnt-umbers, and rich wood browns of late autumn, though the grass was still green underfoot, and the holly and fir trees greener by contrast.

And Peggy was in her element.

Never in all her short life had she been so happy. All the instincts of her Stewart ancestors with their Southern hospitality was finding expression as she led the way to a grove of mighty oaks, tinged by night frosts to the richest maroon, and literally kings of their surroundings, for the deep umber tones of the beeches only served to emphasize their coloring. Beneath them was spread a long table fairly groaning with suggestions of the feast to come, and near it, flanked by Jerome and Mammy, stood Dr. Llewellyn.

As the party came laughing, scrambling or walking toward it he advanced to welcome Mrs. Harold, saying:

"Did you realize that there would be thirteen at the feast unless a fourteenth could be pressed into service? Consider me as merely a necessary adjunct, please, and don't let the young people regard me as a kill-joy because I wear a long coat buttoned straight up to my chin. The only difference really is that I have to keep mine buttoned whereas they have to HOOK THEIR collars," and the good doctor laughed. Introductions followed and then no time was lost in seating the luncheon party.

Then came a moment's pause. Peggy understood and Mrs. Harold's intuition served her. She nodded to Dr. Llewellyn, and none there ever forgot the light which illumined the fine old face as he bowed his head and said softly in his beautifully modulated voice as though speaking to a loved companion.

"Father, for a world so beautiful, for a day so perfect, for the joy and privilege of association with these young people, and the new life which they infuse into ours, we older ones thank Thee. Bring into their lives all that is finest, truest, purest and best - true manhood and womanhood. Amen."

Not a boy or girl but felt the beauty of those simple words and remembered them for many a day.

The grove was not far enough from the house to chance the ruin of any of Aunt Cynthia's dainties. A grassy path led straight to it from her kitchen and at the conclusion of Dr. Llewellyn's grace Peggy nodded slightly to Jerome who in turn nodded to Mammy Lucy, who passed the nod along to some invisible individual, the series of nods bringing about a result which nearly wrecked the dignity of the entire party, for out from behind the long brick building in which Aunt Cynthia ruled supreme, filed a row of little darkies each burdened with a dish, each bare-footed, each immaculate in little white shirt and trousers, each solemnly rolling eyes, the whites of which rivaled his shirt, and each under Cynthia's dire threat of having his "haid busted wide open if he done tripped or spilled a thing," walking as though treading upon eggs.

Along they came, their eyes fixed upon Jerome, for literally they were "between the devil and the deep sea," Jerome and Cynthia being at the beginning and end of that path. Jerome and Mammy received and placed each steaming dish, the very personification of dignity, and in nowise disconcerted by the titter, which soon broke into a full-lunged shout, at the piccaninnies' solemn faces.

It was all too much for good Captain Pennell and the boys, and any "ice" which might possibly have congealed the party, was then and there smashed to smithereens.

"Great! Great!" shouted Captain Pennell, clapping his hands like a boy.

"Eh, this is going some," cried Happy.

"Bully for Chatelaine Peggy!" was Wheedles' outburst.

"Who says Severndale isn't all right?" echoed Ralph.

"Peggy, this is simply delicious," praised Mrs. Harold.

Peggy glowed and Jerome and Mammy beamed, while the little darkies beat a grinning retreat to confide excitedly to Aunt Cynthia:

"Dem gemmens an' ladies yonder in de grove was so mighty pleased dat dey jist nachally bleiged fer ter holler and laugh."

Far from proving drawbacks to the feast the captain and the doctor entered heart and soul into the frolic, the doctor as host, slyly nodding to the ever alert Jerome or Mammy to replenish plates, the captain waxing reminiscent and telling many an amusing tale, and Mrs. Harold beaming happily upon all, while to and from Cynthia's realm ran the little darkies full of enthusiasm for "dem midshipmen mens who suah could eat fried chicken, corn fritters, glazed sweet 'taters, and waffles nuff fer ter bust most mens."

Certainly, Aunt Cynthia knew her business and if ever a picnic feast was appreciated, that one was.

But the climax came with the dessert.

CHAPTER VIII

A SHOCKING DEMONSTRATION OF INTEMPERANCE

The merrymaking was at its height. The festive board had been cleared for dessert.

"Cleared for action," Captain Pennell said.

"Not heavy fire I hope," sighed Shortie. "Peggy, will you excuse me, but I have surely got to let out a reef if anything more is coming," and Shortie let out a hole or two in the leather belt which encircled the region into which innumerable waffles had disappeared.

"There are others; yes there are CERTAINLY others," laughed the captain. "Peggy, my child, to play Circe and still smile is absolutely cruel. The ancient Circe frowned upon her victims."

"And how can I swallow another morsel," was Polly's wail. "Peggy Stewart, why will you have so many good things all at once? Couldn't you have spread it out over several meals and let us have it on the instalment plan?"

"Wheedles couldn't have his birthday that way," laughed Peggy, unwittingly letting a cat escape from a bag, for woe upon the midshipman whose birthday is known. Thus far Wheedles had kept it a profound secret, and Mrs. Harold and Polly, who were wise to what was likely to happen to him if it were known, had kept mum. But, alack, they had forgotten to warn Peggy and her words touched off the mine.

"Eh? What? Never! Something doing? You're a sly one. Thought you'd get off scot-free, did you? Not on your sweet life! Let's give him what for. Excuse this digression, Peggy; it's a ceremony never omitted. It would have been attended to earlier in the day had we suspected, and it can't be delayed any longer. Besides we MUST shake down that which has gone before if more is to follow. Beg pardon, Little Mother, but you know the traditions. Make our peace with Dr. Llewellyn for this little side-show," and the next second Wheedles was in full flight with all his chums hotfoot upon his trail.

How in the world those boys could run as they did after such a feast without apoplexy following, must remain a mystery to all excepting those who have lived in their midst.

Over the lawn, dodging behind the oaks, vaulting the fence into the adjoining field, to the consternation of half a dozen sleek, sedate Alderney cows, tore Wheedles, his pursuers determined to overhand him and administer the drubbing incident to the iniquity of having a birthday.

Dr. Llewellyn and Captain Pennell rose to their feet, one shouting, the other yelling with the rest of the mob, while Mrs. Harold and the girls could only sit and laugh helplessly.

Gabrielle E. Jackson

It was Shortie's long legs which overtook the quarry, both coming to the ground with a crash which would have killed outright any one but a football tackle and a basket-ball captain. In a second the whole bunch had the laughing, helpless victim.

"Look the other way please, people," called Shortie, promptly placing Wheedles across his knee - two men holding his arms, two more his kicking legs - while Shortie properly and deliberately administered twenty sounding spanks. Then releasing him he said to the others who were nothing loath:

"Finish the job. I've done my part and I've had one corking big feed."

And they finished it by holding poor Wheedles by his shoulders and feet and bumping him upon the grass until he must have seen stars - AND THE DINNER WAS WELL SHAKEN DOWN.

"NOW will you try to get away from us?" they demanded, putting him upon his feet.

"It's all over but the shouting, Little Mother, and we'll be good," they laughed as they trooped back to the table, settling blouses, and giving hasty pats to their dishevelled pates, for Wheedles had certainly given them a run for their money.

Meanwhile, Jerome and Mammy had looked on half in consternation, half in glee, for where is your pure-blooded African, old or young, who doesn't sympathize with monkey-shines? As the administrators of justice were in the midst of their self-imposed duties, the half-dozen little darky servitors appeared around the corner of the house bearing the dessert, and there is no telling what might have happened to it had not Aunt Cynthia, hearing the uproar, and "cravin' fer ter know ef de rown' worl' was a-comin' to an end," followed close behind her satellites. That great mold of ice cream, mound of golden wine jelly, dishes of cakes galore would certainly have met total destruction but for her prompt and emphatic command:

"Yo' chillern 'tend to yo' bisness an' nemmine what gwine on over yander." That saved the feast, for the little darkies were convinced that "one ob dose young mens liked ter be kill fer suah."

Had it been mid-July instead of a Maryland November that ice cream could not have vanished more quickly, and in the process of its disappearance, Jerome vanished also. This was not noticed by Peggy's guests, but his return was hailed with first a spontaneous shout and then a:

"Rah! Rah! Hoohrah! Hoohrah! Navy Hoohrah!" and "Oh that's some cake!" "Nothing the matter with THAT edifice." "Who said we couldn't eat any more?" For with the dignity of a majordomo Jerome bore upon its frilled paper doily a huge chocolate layer cake, ornately decorated with yellow icing, and twenty dark blue candles, their yellow flames barely flickering in the still air, while behind him walked his little trenchermen, one bearing a big glass pitcher of amber cider, another, dishes of nuts, and another a tray of Mammy Lucy's home-made candies.

If ever a birthday cake was enjoyed and appreciated, certainly that one was, and there is no telling how long the merry party would have lingered over the nuts, candies and cider had not a startling interruption taken place.

The afternoon was well advanced. Mrs. Harold, the captain and Dr. Llewellyn had reached the limit of their appetites and were now watching and listening to the merry chatter of the young people who sat sipping the cider - they had long since passed beyond the DRINKING point - and eating the black walnuts and hickory nuts which had been gathered upon the estate, for Severndale was famous for its cider and nuts. The cider was made from a brand of apples which had been grown in the days of Peggy's great-grandfather and carefully cultivated for years. They ripened late, and needed a touch of frost to perfect them. The ciderhouse and press stood just beyond the meadow in which the Severndale cows led a luxurious life of it, and the odor of the rich fruit invariably drew a line of them to the dividing fence, where they sniffed and peered longingly at "forbidden fruit." But if every dog, as we are told, has his day, certainly a cow may hope to have hers some time. That it should have happened to be Wheedles' day also was merely accidental.

As in most respectable communities there is almost invariably an individual or two whose conduct is open to criticism, so in Severndale's eminently irreproach- able herd of sleek kine there was one obstreperous creature and her offspring. They were possessed to do the things their more well conducted sisters never thought of doing. The cow had a strain of distinctly plebian blood which, transmitted to her calf, probably accounted for their eccentricities. If ever a fence was broken through, if ever a brimming pail of milk was overturned, if a stable towel was chewed to ribbons, a feed bin rifled, it could invariably be traced to Betsy

Brindle and her incorrigible daughter Sally Simple, and this afternoon they surpassed themselves. As Peggy's guests sat in that blissful state of mind and body resulting from being "serenely full, the epicure would say," they were startled by an altogether rowdy, abandoned "Moo-oo-oo-oo," echoed in a higher key, and over the lawn came two as disreputable-looking animals as one could picture, for Betsy Brindle and her daughter, a pretty little year-old heifer, were unquestionably, undeniably, hopelessly intoxicated. Betsy was swaying and staggering from side to side, wagging her head foolishly and mooing in the most maudlin manner, while Sally, whose potations affected her quite differently, was cavorting madly thither and yonder, one moment almost standing upon her head, with hind legs and tail waving wildly in mid-air, the next with the order reversed and pawing frantically at the clouds.

Behind the arrant ones in mad chase and consternation came the young negro lad whose duty it was to see that the cattle were properly housed at nightfall. He had gone to the meadow for his charges only to find these incorrigibles, as upon many another occasion, missing. How long they had been at large he could not guess. At last, after long search, he discovered them in the inclosure where the barreled apples were kept and two whole barrels rifled. When this had taken place his African mind did not analyze, though a scientist could have told him almost to an hour and explained also that in the cows' double stomachs the apples had promptly fermented and become highly intoxicating, with the present result. But poor Cicero was petrified. His young mistress entertaining "de quality" and his unruly charges scandalizing her by tearing into their very midst.

"Moo - o - moo, e - moooo - " bellowed Betsy, making snake tracks across the lawn.

"Moo, Moo, Moo, Moo, Mooee - " echoed Sally in lively staccato, doing a wild Highland fling with quite original steps.

"Hi dar! Come 'long away. Get off en dat lawn. Come away from dat 'ar pa'ty," screamed Cicero. "Ma Lawd-a-mighty, dem cows gwine 'grace me an' ruin me fer evah," and it would doubtless have proved true had not the boys sprung to their feet to join in the cowherd's duties, only too ready for any prank which presented an outlet for their fun-loving souls. Shortie promptly took command of the defending forces, and crying:

"Come on, fellows, head the old lady off before she knocks the table endwise," was off with a rush, the others hotfoot after him, waving arms and shouting until poor old Betsy Brindle's addled head must have thought all the imps of the lower regions turned loose upon her. Circling wide, the boys made a complete barrier beyond which the poor tipsy cow dared not force her way. So with a hopelessly pathetic "moo" and a look at her adversaries which might have done credit to the mock turtle of Lewis Carrol's creation, she surrendered forthwith, and promptly flopped down in the middle of the lawn.

Not so her daughter. Not a bit of it! SHE had not finished her fling and never did madder chase ensue than the one which at length ended in effectually cornering the flighty one.

"Lemme tote her home. Fer de Lawd's sake, sah, lemme tote her home quick, 'fore Unc' Jess an' Missie

Peggy kill me daid," begged Cicero.

"You tote her home, you spindly little shaver! She'd part her cable and go adrift in half a minute after you got under way. Come on, boys, we've got to convoy this craft into her home port. Make fast," and with the experience of three years' training in seamanship, Shortie and his companions proceeded to make fast the recalcitrate Sally, and amidst hoots and yells calculated to sober up the most hopeless inebriate, they led her to her barn where Cicero read her the riot act as he fastened her in her stall. Meanwhile Betsy had succumbed to slumber and at Dr. Llewellyn's suggestion was left to sleep off the effects of her over-indulgence. When the boys got back from the barn poor Peggy was run unmercifully.

"And we thought Severndale a model home. A well-conducted establishment. Yet the very first time we come out here we find even the COWS with a jag on that a confirmed toper couldn't equal if he tried, and yet you pose as a model young woman, Peggy Stewart, and are accepted in all good faith as our Captain Polly's friend. Watch out, Little Mother. Watch out. We can't let our little Captain visit where even the COWS give way to such disgraceful performances."

Poor Peggy was incapable of defending herself for she and Polly had laughed until they were weak, and for many a long day after Peggy heard of her tipsy cows.

When peace once more descended upon the land it was almost time for the visitors to return to Annapolis, but before departing they visited the paddock, the stables, and the beautiful old colonial house. And so ended Wheedles' birthday, and the next excitement was caused by the Army-Navy game to which Peggy went with Mrs. Harold's party, enjoying the outing as only a girl whose experiences have been limited, and who is ready for new impressions, can enjoy. And with the passing of the game November passed also and before she knew it Christmas was upon her, and Christmas hitherto for Peggy had meant merely gifts from Daddy Neil and a merrymaking for the servants. Without manifesting undue curiosity Mrs. Harold had learned a good deal concerning Peggy's life and nothing she had learned had touched her so deeply as the loneliness of the holiday season for the young girl. It seemed to her the most unnatural she had ever heard of, and something like resentment filled her heart when she thought of Neil Stewart's unconscious neglect of his little daughter. She argued that his failing to appreciate that he was neglectful did not excuse the fact, and she resolved that this year Peggy should spend the holidays with her and Polly at Wilmot, and the servants at Severndale could look to their own well-being. Nevertheless, Peggy laid her plans for the pleasure of the Severndale help and saw to it that they would have a happy time under Harrison's supervision. Then Peggy betook herself to Wilmot for the happiest Christmastide she had ever known.

The holiday season at the Academy is always a merry one, but until very recently, there has been no Christmas recess and the midshipmen had to find amusement right in the little old town of Annapolis, or within the Academy's limits. The frolicking begins with the Christmas eve hop given by the midshipmen.

Mrs. Harold had not allowed Polly to attend the hops given earlier in the winter, for she was a wise woman and felt that social diversions of that nature were best reserved for later years, when school-days were ended. But she made an exception at the Christmas season, when Polly in common with other girls, had a holiday, and Peggy and Polly would go to the hop.

Unless one has seen a hop given at the Academy it is difficult to understand the beauty of the scene, and to Peggy it seemed a veritable fairy-land, with its lights, its banners, its lovely girls, uniformed laddies and music "which would make a wooden image dance," she confided to Mrs. Harold, and added: "And do you know, I used to rebel and be so cranky when Miss Arnaud came to give me dancing-lessons when I was a little thing. I just HATED it, and how she ever made me learn I just don't know. But I had to do as she said, and maybe I'm not glad that I DID. Why, Little Mother, suppose I HADN'T learned. Wouldn't I have been ashamed of myself now?"

Mrs. Harold pulled a love-lock as she answered: "You train your colts, girlie, and they are the better for their training, aren't they?"

Peggy gave a quick glance of comprehension, and her lips curved in a smile as she said:

"But they never behave half as badly as I used to with Miss Arnaud."

And so the Christmas eve was danced away.

Christmas morning was the merriest Peggy had ever known. Long before daylight she was wakened by Polly shaking her and crying:

"Peggy, wake up! Wake up! What do you think? Aunt

Janet has filled stockings and hung them on the foot of the bed. She must have slipped in while we were sound asleep, and oh, I don't wonder we slept after that dance, do you?" rattled on Polly, scrambling around to close the window and turn on the steam, for the morning was a snappy one.

"Whow! Ooo!" yawned Peggy, to whom late hours were a novelty and who felt as though she had dropped asleep only ten minutes before. "Why, Polly Howland, it's pitch dark, and midnight! I know it is," she protested. "How do you know there are stockings there, anyway?"

"I was shivering and when I reached over to get the puff cover my hand touched something bumpy. I've felt of it and I KNOW it's a stocking. I never thought of having one, for I thought all those things were way back in little girl days. But turn on the electric lights quick - they're on your side of the bed - and we'll see what's in them; the stockings, I mean."

Peggy turned the button and the lights flashed up.

"Goodness, isn't it freezing cold," she cried. "Let's put the puff cover around us," and rolled up in the big down coverlet the girls dove into their bumpy stockings, exclaiming or laughing over the contents, for evidently the boys had been in the secret, for out of Peggy's came a little bronze cow and calf labeled "C. and S."

"Now what in the world does C. and S. stand for, I wonder?" she said.

"Oh, Peggy, those are the initials for 'Clean and Sober,'

the report the officer-of-the-deck makes when the enlisted men come aboard after being on liberty. If they are intoxicated and untidy they check them up D. and D. - which means Drunk and Dirty. You'll never hear the last of Betsy Brindle's caper."

"Well look and see what they've run you about, for you won't escape, I'll wager," laughed Peggy as merrily as though it were broad daylight instead of five A.M.

Polly dove into her stocking to fish out a tiny rocking horse with a doll riding astride it. The horse was to all intents and purposes on a mad gallop, for his rider's hair, DYED A VIVID RED, was streaming out behind, her collar was flying loose, her feet were out of the stirrups and one shoe was gone. The mad rider bore the legend:

"Lady Gilpin."

A dozen other nonsensical things followed, but down in the toe of each was a beautiful 19 - class pin for each of the girls, with "Co-ed 19 - " engraved on them and cards saying "with the compliments of the bunch."

By the time the stockings' contents were investigated it was time to dress and go with Mrs. Harold to see the Christmas Parade, always given before breakfast in Bancroft Hall and through the Yard. Mrs. Harold tapped upon the girls' door and was greeted with "Merry Christmas! Merry Christmas!" She entered, taking them in her arms and saying:

"Dozens and dozens for each of you, my little foster-daughters. I am so glad to have you with me, for Christmas isn't Christmas without young people to enjoy it, and I think I've got some of the very sweetest and best to be had - both daughters and sons. There are no more children like my foster-children. I am one lucky old lady."

"Old!" cried Peggy indignantly, "Why you'll never, never seem old to us, for you just think, and see, and feel every single thing as we do."

"That's a pretty compliment," replied Mrs. Harold, sealing her words with a kiss which was returned with earnest warmth, for Peggy was learning to love this friend very dearly.

The Christmas Parade was funny enough, for the midshipmen had sent to Philadelphia for their costumes and every living thing, from Fiji Islanders, to priests, bears, lions, ballet girls or convicts raced through the Yard to the music of "Tommy's band" as they called the ridiculous collection of wind instruments over which one of the midshipmen waved his baton as bandmaster.

When this great show ended, all hurried away to dress for breakfast formation, for many were the invitations to breakfast with friends out in town, legal holidays being the only days upon which such privileges were allowed. Mrs. Harold had a party of five beside Polly and Peggy and the griddle cakes which vanished that morning rivaled the number of waffles which had disappeared at Severndale. When breakfast ended Mrs. Harold said:

"Can you young people give me about two hours out of your day? Polly and I have laid a little plan for someone's pleasure, which we know will be enhanced if you boys cooperate with us."

"Count on us, Little Mother."

"We'll do anything we can for you, for you do enough for us."

"Sure thing," were the hearty replies, while Peggy slipped to her side to whisper: "I'd almost be willing to give up my 'Co-ed' class pin if you asked me to."

"No such sacrifice as that, honey. But let's all go up to Middies' Haven where I'll tell you all about it."

CHAPTER IX

DUNMORE'S LAST CHRISTMAS

When Mrs. Harold's little breakfast party returned to her sitting-room, she dropped into her favorite chair before the blazing log fire, motioning to the others to gather about her. Polly and Peggy promptly perched upon the arms of her chair, nestling close; Durand squatted, Turk-fashion, upon a big cushion at her feet. Wheedles leaned with unstudied grace against the mantel-shelf, while Happy, Ralph, and Shortie seated themselves upon the big couch whose capacity seemed to be something like the magic tent of the Arabian Nights' tale, and capable of indefinite expansion.

"What is it, Little Mother?" asked Wheedles, while Durand glanced up with his deep, dark eyes, and a slight quiver of the sensitive mouth.

"Just a little plan I have for Dunmore's happiness today" she answered, alluding to a second-classman who had been severely injured upon the football field late in October, and who had been paralyzed ever since. His people lived far away and it was difficult for them to reach him, and the day would have been a sad one but for his chums in the Academy and his many friends.

Among these latter none were more devoted than Mrs. Harold and Polly, for Lewis Dunmore had been one of the Little Mother's boys since he first entered the Academy and she was nearly heart-broken at the serious outcome of his accident, as no hope was entertained of his recovery.

All knew this, and the tenderest sympathy went out to the sick lad who had never for a moment ceased to hope for ultimate recovery and whose patience, courage and cheerfulness under conditions so terrible, filled with admiration the hearts of all who knew him.

Polly had been untiring in her devotion to him, and "the little foster-sister," as he called her, spent many an hour in the hospital, reading, talking, or whistling like a bird, for whistling was Polly's sole accomplishment. Peggy often went with her, for she loved to make others happy, and many a weary hour was made less weary for him by the two girls, and Peggy had sent many a dainty dish from Severndale, or the fruit and flowers for which it was noted. She knew Polly and Mrs. Howland had planned something for Christmas day, but waited for them to tell her, feeling delicate about asking questions. She had sent over every dainty she could think of and great bunches of mistletoe.

Mrs. Harold smiled upon the young faces she loved so dearly and said

"Yesterday morning Polly and I sent up a lot of Christmas greens and a tree for Lewis, and later went up to dress it, arranging with the nurses to put it in his room when he was sleeping that it might be the first thing his eyes fell upon when he wakened this morning. He has probably been looking at it many an hour, but we told the nurses we would come up about ten-thirty to give him the presents. We wanted to make it a merry hour for him, and so a lot of nonsensical things were put on for his friends also, among them you boys and some others to whom I have written, and who will meet us there. Can you join us?"

"Can we! Well why not? Sure! Poor old chap!" were some of the hearty responses.

"I knew I could count upon you, so let us start at once. Go get ready, girls."

The girls flew to their room and a moment later came back coated and furred, for the walk up to the hospital on the hill was a bleak one. The boys were inured to all sorts of weather, and their heavy overcoats were a safe protection against it. It was a merry, frolicking party which set forth, and as they crossed the athletic field a lively snowballing took place, for a light snow had fallen the day before, turning the Yard into a beautiful white world.

Mrs. Harold was not to be outdone by any of her young people, but catching up handfuls of snow in her woolen-gloved hands tossed snowballs with the best of them.

The contrast from the joy, the vigorous health of the group entering Dunmore's room to the still, helpless figure lying upon the cot was pathetic. The invalid could not move his head, but his great brown eyes, and fine mouth smiled his welcome to his friends, and he said:

"Oh, it was great! Great! I saw it the first thing when I

woke up. And the holly and mistletoe up here over my bed. I don't see how they got it hung there without my knowing when they did it."

"That was our secret," cried Polly. "And Peggy sent over the mistletoe from Severndale, though she didn't know we were to have the tree."

"Peggy, you are all right," was Dunmore's hearty praise. "But that tree is the prettiest thing ever. I'm as crazy as a kid about it. I sort of dreaded Christmas, but you people have fixed it up all right and I'm no end grateful. It's a great day after all."

Peggy who was standing where Dunmore could not see her glanced at Polly. Polly nodded in quick understanding. "The day all right," and the poor lad helpless as some lifeless thing. The girls' eyes filled with quick tears which they hastened to wink away, for not for worlds would they have saddened what both knew to be the last Christmas Lewis could pass in this world, and Polly cried:

"Now, Tanta, let us have the presents!" For an hour the room was the scene of a happy merrymaking, as Shortie, because he was "built on lines to reach the top-gallants," they said, distributed the gifts, funny or dainty, and Lewis' bed looked like a stand in a bazaar. Mrs. Harold had given him a downy bathrobe; Peggy had made him a hop pillow; Polly had made up a nonsense jingle for each day for a month, sealing each in an envelope and labelling it with dire penalties if read before the date named.

But best of all, the class had sent him his class-ring and when it was slipped upon his finger by his roommate, the poor lad broke down completely.

Mrs. Harold hastened to the bedside and the others did their best to relieve the situation.

The class-ring is never worn by a second-classman until the last exam is passed by the first class. Then the new class-rings blossom forth in all their glory, for this ring is peculiarly significant: It is looked forward to as one of the greatest events in the class' history, and is a badge of union forever.

Realizing that Dunmore could not be with them when the time came for them to put on their own, his classmates had unanimously voted to give him his as a Christmas gift, and nothing they could have done could possibly have meant so much to him. He was prouder than he had ever been before in his life, but - with the gift came the faint premonition of the inevitable; the first doubt of future recovery; the first hint that perhaps he had been harboring false hopes, and it almost overwhelmed him, and Mrs. Harold read it all in a flash. But Peggy saved the day. Slipping to his side she said:

"Aren't you proud to be the very first to wear it? They wanted to give you a Christmas present, but couldn't think of a single thing you'd enjoy while you were so ill. Then they thought of the ring. Of course you could enjoy THAT, and there was no reason in the world that you shouldn't either, and the other boys will be happy seeing you wear it and count the days before they can put theirs on. And it is such a beauty, isn't it? We are all so glad you've got it. You can just wiggle your finger and crow over the others every time they come to visit you."

Lewis looked up at her and smiled. He understood better than she guessed why she had talked so fast, and was grateful, but the pang was beneath the smile nevertheless.

Then dinner-hour drawing near the white-capped nurse came in as a gentle hint that her patient had had about all the excitement he could stand, and Mrs. Harold suggested their departure. Their last glance showed them Lewis Dunmore looking at his class-ring, for he could move that arm just enough to enable him to raise the hand within his range of vision.

The week following was a happy one for all. Each afternoon an informal dance was given in the gymnasium and the girls pranced to their hearts' content. As the week drew to an end the weather grew colder and colder until with Saturday came a temperature which froze College Creek solid. This was most unusual for the season, but was hailed with wild rejoicings by the boys and girls, for skating is a rare novelty in Annapolis.

Saturday dawned an ideal winter day, clear, cold, and white.

"Can you skate, Peggy?" asked Polly, diving into her closet for a pair of skates which she had brought South with her, though with small hope of using them.

"Y - e - s," answered Peggy, doubtfully. "I can skate - after a fashion, but I'm afraid my skating will not show to very great advantage beside yours, you Northern lassie."

" Nonsense. I'll wager one of Aunt Cynthia's cookies

that you can skate as well as I can, though you never would admit it."

There had not been much chance for stirring exercise for the girls since the snow fell and really cold weather set in, for there was not much pleasure in riding under such conditions, and they had both missed the healthy outdoor sport. But the prospect of skating set them both a-tingle to get upon the ice and they were eagerly awaiting the official order from the Academy, for no one is allowed upon the ice until it is pronounced entirely safe by the authorities, and the Commandant gives permission. Of course, this does not apply to the townspeople or to that section of the creek beyond the limits of the Academy, but it is very rigidly enforced within it. As the girls were eager to learn whether the brigade would have permission that afternoon, they went over to hear the orders read at luncheon formation, and came back nearly wild with delight to inform Mrs. Harold that not only was permission granted but that the band would play at the edge of the creek from four until six o'clock.

"And if THAT won't be ideal I'd like to know what can be," cried Polly, and scarcely had she spoken when the telephone rang.

"Hello. Yes, it's Polly. Of course we can. What time! To the very minute. Yes, Peggy's right here beside me and fairly dancing up and down to know what we are talking about. No, don't come out for us; we will meet you at the gate at three-thirty sharp. Good-bye," and snapping the receiver into its socket, Polly whirled about to catch Peggy in a regular bear hug and cry:

" It was Happy. He and the others want us ALL to

come over at three-thirty. Aunt Janet, too. They have an ice-chair for her; they borrowed it from someone. Oh, won't it be fun!"

Peggy's dark eyes sparkled, then she said: "But my skates. They are 'way out at Severndale."

Without a word Mrs. Harold walked to the telephone and a moment later was talking with Harrison. The skates would be sent in by the two o'clock car. Promptly at three-thirty the girls and Mrs. Harold entered the Maryland Avenue gate where they were met by Shortie, Wheedles, Happy, Durand and Ralph; Durand promptly appropriating Peggy, while Ralph, cried:

"Come on, Polly, this is going to be like old times up at Montgentian."

It would have been hard to picture a prettier sight than the skaters presented that afternoon, the boys in their heavy reefers and woolen watch-caps; the girls in toboggan caps and sweaters. Over in the west the sky was a rich rosy glow, for the sun sinks behind the hills by four-thirty during the short winter afternoons. The Naval Academy band stationed at the edge of the broad expanse of the ice-bound creek was sending its inspiring strains out across the keen, frosty air which seemed to hold and toy with each note as though reluctant to let it die away.

The boys took turns in pushing Mrs. Harold's chair, spinning it along over the smooth surface of the ice in the wake of Peggy, Polly and the others, who now and again joined hands to "snap-the-whip," "run-the-train," or go through some pretty figure. Polly and Ralph were clever at this and very soon Peggy caught the trick. The creek was crowded, for nearly half the town as well as the people from the Yard were enjoying the rare treat.

The band had just finished a beautiful waltz to which all had swung across the creek in perfect rhythm, when one of the several enlisted men, stationed along the margin of the creek, and equipped with stout ropes and heavy planks in the event of accident, sounded "attention" on a bugle. Instantly, every midshipman, officer, or those in any way connected with the Academy, halted and stood at attention to hear the order.

"No one will be allowed to go below the bridge. Ice is not safe," rang out the order.

Nearly every one heard and to hear was, of course, to obey for all in the Academy, but there are always heedless ones, or stupid ones in this world, and in the numbers gathered upon the ice that afternoon there were plenty of that sort, and it sometimes seems as though they were sent into this world to get sensible people into difficulties. Of course the heedless ones were too busy with their own concerns to pay heed to the warning. A group of young girls from the town were skating together close to the lower bridge. Durand and Peggy were near the Marine Barracks shore, when they became aware of their reckless venturing upon the dangerous ice.

"Durand, look," cried Peggy. "Those girls must be crazy to go out there after hearing that order."

"They probably never heard it at all. Some of those cits

make me tired. They seem to have so little sense. Now I'll bet my sweater that every last person connected with the Yard heard it, but, I'd bet TWO sweaters that not half the people from the town did, yet there was no reason they shouldn't. It was read for their benefit just exactly as much as ours, but they act as though we belonged to some other world and the orders were for our benefit, but their undoing."

"Not quite so bad as all that, I hope," laughed Peggy, as they joined hands and swung away. A moment later she gave a sharp cry. Durand had turned and was skating backward with Peggy "in tow." He spun around just in time to see a little girl about ten years of age throw up her hands and crash through the rotten ice. Peggy had seen her as she laughingly broke away from the group of older girls to dart beneath the bridge.

"Quick! Beat it for help," shouted Durand, flinging off his reefer and striking out for the screaming girls. He had not made ten strides when a second girl in rushing to her friend's assistance, went through too, the others darting back to safer ice and shrieking for help. Durand now had a proposition on hand in short order, but Peggy's wits worked rapidly: If she left Durand to go for help he would have his hands more than full. Moreover, the alarm had already been sounded and the Jackies were coming on a run. So she did exactly as Durand was doing: laid flat upon the ice and worked her way toward the second struggling victim. Durand had caught the child and was doing his best to keep her afloat and himself from being dragged into the freezing water, but Peggy's victim was older and heavier.

"Oh, save me! Save me!" she screamed.

"Hush. Keep still and we'll get you out," commanded Peggy, doing her utmost to keep free of the wildly thrashing arms, while holding on to the girl's coat with all the strength of desperation. It would have gone ill with the girl and Peggy, however, had not help come from the bridge where the Jackies had acted as such men invariably do: promptly and without fuss. In far less time than seemed possible, two of them, with ropes firmly bound about their bodies, were in the water, while two more pulled them and their struggling charges to safety, and two more in the perfect order of their discipline drew Peggy and Durand from their perilous situation, and just then Mrs. Harold's party came rushing up, she and Polly white with terror.

"Peggy, Peggy, my little girl! If anything had happened to you," cried Mrs. Harold, gathering her into her arms.

"But there hasn't. Not a single thing, Little Mother. I'm not hurt a bit, and only a little wet and that won't hurt me because my clothes are so thick." But the girl's voice shook and she trembled in spite of her words, for the last few minutes had taxed both strength and courage.

Meantime the boys had gathered about Durand, but boy-like made light of the episode though down in their hearts they knew it had required pluck and steady nerve to do as he had done, and their admiration found expression in hauling off their reefers to force them upon him, or in giving him a clip upon the back and telling him he was "all right," and to "come on back to Bancroft for a rub-down after his bath." But no one underrated the courage of either and they were hurried home to be cared for, though it was many hours before Mrs. Harold could throw off the horror of what might have happened, and Peggy was a heroine for many a day to her intense annoyance.

Gabrielle E. Jackson

CHAPTER X

A DOMESTIC EPISODE

In spite of the scare all had received the previous Saturday, the New Year's eve hop was thoroughly enjoyed, for neither Durand nor Peggy was the worse for the experience, and the old year was danced out upon light, happy toes, only one shadow resting upon the joyous evening.

For over a year, there had been an officer stationed at the Academy who had been a source of discord among his fellow-officers, and a martinet with the midshipmen. He was small, petty, unjust, and not above resorting to methods despised by his confreres. He was loathed by the midshipmen because they could never count upon what they termed "a square deal," and consequently never knew just where they stood.

There were several who seemed to have incurred his especial animosity, and Durand in particular he hated: hated because the boy's quick wits invariably got him out of the scrapes which his mischievous spirit prompted, and "Gumshoes," as the boys had dubbed the officer, owing to his habit of sneaking about "looking for trouble," was not clever enough to catch him.

And thus it came about that, being once more circumvented by Durand on New Year's eve in a trivial matter at which any other officer would have laughed, he resorted to ways and means which a man with a finer sense of honor would have despised and - again he failed. But his chance came on New Year's day, when Durand, led into one of the worst scrapes of his life by Blue, fell into his clutches and the outcome was so serious that the entire brigade was restricted to the Yard's limits for three months, and gloom descended not only upon the Academy but upon all its friends.

Naturally, with her boys debarred from Middies' Haven, Mrs. Harold could do little for the girls, and their only sources of pleasure lay in such amusements as the town afforded and these were extremely limited. So much time was spent at Severndale with Peggy, and it was during one of these visits that Mrs. Harold figured in one of the domestic episodes of Severndale. They were not new to Peggy for she was Southern-born and used to the vagaries and childlike outbreaks of the colored people. But even though Mrs. Harold had lived among them a great deal, and thought she understood them pretty thoroughly, she had yet to learn some of the African's eccentricities.

January dragged on, the girls working with Captain Pennell and Dr. Llewellyn. During the month, one of the hands, Joshua Jozadak Jubal Jones, by the way, fell ill with typhoid fever, and was removed to the hospital. From the first his chances of recovery seemed doubtful, and "Minervy" his wife, as strapping, robust a specimen of her race as poor Joshua was tiny and, as she expressed it, "pore and pindlin'," was in a most emotional frame of mind. Again and again she came up to the great house to "crave consolatiom" from Miss

Peggy, or Mammy Lucy, though, truth to tell, Mammy's sympathies were not very deeply enlisted. Minervy Jones did not move in the same SOCIAL SET in which Mammy held a dignified position: Mammy was "an emerged Baptis'"; Minervy a "Shoutin' Mefodist," and a strong feeling existed between the two little colored churches. Peggy visited the hospital daily and saw that Joshua lacked for nothing. Mrs. Harold was deeply concerned for Peggy's sake, for Peggy looked to the well-being of all the help upon the estate with the deep interest which generations of her ancestors had manifested, indeed regarded as incumbent upon them and part of their obligation to their dependents.

Days passed and poor Joshua grew no better, Minervy meanwhile spending most of her time in Aunt Cynthia's kitchen where she could sustain the inner woman with many a tidbit from the white folks' table, and speculate upon what was likely to become of them if her "pore lil chillern were left widderless orphans." It need hardly be added that the prospective "widderless orphans" were left to shift largely for themselves while she was accepting both mental and physical sustenance.

It was upon one of these visits, so indefinitely prolonged that Mammy's patience was at the snapping point, that she decided to give a needed hint. Entering the kitchen she said to Aunt Cynthia:

"'Pears ter me yo' must have powerful lot o' time on han', Sis' Cynthy."

"Well'm I AIN'T. No ma'am, not me," was Cynthia's prompt reply, for to tell the truth she was beginning to weary of doling out religious consolation and bodily sustenance, yet hospitality demanded something.

"Well, I reckons Miss Peggy's cravin' fer her luncheon, an' it's high time she done got it, too. Is yo' know de time?"

"Cou'se I knows de time," brindled Cynthia, "but 'pears lak time don' count wid some folks. Kin YO' see de clock, Mis' Jones?"

The question was sprung so suddenly that Minerva jumped.

"Yas'm, yas'm, Mis' Johnson, I kin see hit; yis, I kin," answered Minervy, craning her neck for a pretended better view.

"Well, den, please, ma'am, tell me just 'zactly what it IS."

This was a poser. Minervy knew no more of telling time than one of her own children, but rising from her chair, she said:

"I 'clar ter goodness, I'se done shed so many tears in ma sorrer and grief over Joshua dat I sho' is a-loosin' ma eyesight." She then went close to the clock, looked long and carefully at it, but shook her head doubtfully. At length a bright idea struck her and turning to Cynthia she announced:

"Why, Sis' Cynthia, I believes yo' tryin' ter projec' wid me; dat clock don' STRIKE 'TALL. But I 'clar I mus' be a-humpin' masef todes dera chillern. I shore mus'."

"Yes, I'd 'vise it pintedly," asserted Cynthia, while Mammy Lucy added:

"It's sprisin' how some folks juties slips dey min's."

Three days later word came to Severndale that Joshua could hardly survive the day and Peggy, as she felt duty bound, went over to Minervy's cabin. She found her sitting before her fire absolutely idle.

"Minervy," she began, "I have had word from the hospital and Joshua is not so well. I think you would better go right over."

"Yas'm, yas'm, Miss Peggy, I spec's yo' sees it dat-a-way, honey, but - but yo' sees de chillern dey are gwine car'y on scan'lus if I leaves 'em. My juty sho' do lie right hyer, yas'm it sho' do."

"But Minervy, Joshua cannot live."

"Yas'm, but he ain' in his min' an' wouldn't know me no how, but dese hyer chillerns is ALL got dey min's cl'ar, an' dey STUMMICKS empty. No'm, I knows yo' means it kindly an' so I teks hit, but I knows ma juty," and nothing Peggy could say had any effect.

That night Joshua died. The word came to Severndale early the following morning.

"Well," said Mrs. Harold, "from her philosophical resignation to the situation yesterday, I don't imagine she will be greatly overcome by the news."

"Mh - um," was Mammy's non-committal lip-murmur, and Peggy wagged her head. Mrs. Harold and Polly were spending the week at Severndale, and were dressing for breakfast. Their rooms communicated with Peggy's and they had been laughing and talking together when the 'phone message came.

"Mammy," called Peggy. "Please send word right down to Minervy."

"Yas, baby, I sends it, and den yo' watch out," warned Mammy.

"What for?" asked Peggy.

"Fo' dat 'oman. She gwine mak one fuss DIS time ef she never do again."

"Nonsense, Mammy, I don't believe she cares one straw anyway. She is the most unfeeling creature I've ever seen."

"She may be ONfeelin' but she ain' ON-doin', yo' mark me," and Mammy went off to do as she was bidden.

Perhaps twenty minutes had passed when the quiet of the lower floor was torn by wild shrieks and on-rushing footsteps, with voices vainly commanding silence and decorum: commands all unheeded. Then came a final rush up the stairs and Minervy distraught and dishevelled burst into Mrs. Harold's room, and without pausing to see whom she was falling upon, flung her arms about that startled woman, shrieking:

"He's daid! He's daid! Dem pore chillern is all widderless orphans. I felt it a-comin'! Who' gwine feed an' clothe and shelter dose pore lambs? Ma heart's done bruck! Done bruck!"

"Minervy! Minervy! Do you know what you are doing! Let go of Mrs. Harold this instant," ordered Peggy, nearly overcome with mortification that her guest should meet with such an experience at Severndale. "Do you hear me? Control yourself at once."

She strove to drag the hysterical creature from Mrs. Harold, but she might as well have tried to drag away a wild animal. Minervy continued to shriek and howl, while Mammy, scandalized beyond expression, scolded and stormed, and Jerome called from the hall below.

Then Mrs. Harold's sense of humor came to her rescue and she had an inspiration, for she promptly decided that there was no element of grief in Minervy's emotions.

"Minerva, Minerva, HAVE you ordered your mourning? You knew Joshua could not live," she cried.

Had she felled the woman with a blow the effect could not have been more startling. Instantly the shrieks ceased and releasing her hold Minervy struck an attitude:

"No'm, I HASN'T! I cyant think how I could a-been so careless-like, an' knowin' all de endurin' time dat I boun' fer ter be a widder. How could I a-been so light-minded?"

"Well, you have certainly got to have some black clothes right off. It would be dreadful not to have proper mourning for Joshua."

Meanwhile Peggy and Polly had fled into the

next room.

"I sho' mus', ma'am. How could I a-been so 'crastinatin' an' po' Joshua a-dyin' all dese hyer weeks. I am' been 'spectful to his chillern; dat I ain't. Lemme go rightway an' tink what I's needin'. But please ma'am, is YO' a widder 'oman? Case ef yo' is yo's had spurrience an' kin tell me bes' what I needs."

It was with difficulty that Mrs. Harold controlled her risibles, so utterly absurd rather than pathetic was the whole situation, for not one atom of real grief for Joshua lay in poor, shallow Minervy's heart. Then Mrs. Harold replied:

"No, Minervy. I am not a widow; at least I am only a GRASS widow, and they do not wear mourning, you know."

"No'm, no'm, I spec's not. But what mus' I git for masef an' does po' orphans!"

"Well, you have a black skirt, but have you a waist and hat? And you would better buy a black veil; not crape, it is too perishable; get nun's veiling, and - "

"Nun's veilin'? Nun's veilin'?" hesitated Minervy. "But I ain' NO NUN, mistiss, I'se a WIDDER. I ain' got no kind er use fer dem nunses wha' don' never mahry. I'se been a mahryin' 'oman, *I* is."

"Well you must choose your own veil then," Mrs. Harold managed to reply.

"Yas'm, I guesses I better, an' I reckons I better git me a belt an' some shoes, 'case if I gotter be oneasy in ma min' dars no sort o' reason fer ma bein' uneasy in ma FOOTS too, ner dem chillern neither. Dey ain' never is had shoes all 'roun' ter onct, but I reckons dey better he fitted out right fer dey daddy's funeral. Dey can't tend it hut onct in all dey life-times no how. And 'sides, I done had his life assured 'gainst dis occasiom, an' I belongs ter de sassiety wha' burys folks in style wid regalions. Dey all wears purple velvet scaffses ober dey shoulders an' ma'ches side de hearse. Dar ain' nothin' cheap an' no 'count bout DAT sassiety. No ma'am! An' I reckons I better git right long and look arter it all," and Minervy, still wiping her eyes, hurried from the room, Mammy's snort of outrage unheeded, and her words:

"NOW what I done tole yo', baby? I tells yo' dat 'oman ain' mo'n ha'f human if she IS one ob ma own color. I'S a cullured person, but she's jist pure nigger, yo' hyar me?" and Mammy flounced from the room.

Polly and Peggy reentered Mrs. Harold's room. She had collapsed upon the divan, almost hysterical, and Polly looked as though someone had dashed cold water in her face. Peggy was the only one who accepted the situation philosophically. With a resigned expression she said:

"THAT'S Minervy Jones. She is one type of her race. Mammy is another. Now we'll see what she'll buy. I'll venture to say that every penny she gets from Joshua's life-insurance will be spent upon clothes for herself and those children."

"And I started the idea," deplored Mrs. Harold.

"Oh, no, you did not. She would have thought of it as

soon as she was over her screaming, only you stopped the screaming a little sooner, for which we ought to be grateful to you. She is only one of many more exactly like her."

"Do you mean to tell me that there are many as heedless and foolish as she is?" demanded Mrs. Harold.

"Dozens. Ask Harrison about some of them."

"Well, I never saw anything like her," cried Polly, indignantly. "I think she is perfectly heartless."

"Oh, no, she isn't. She simply can't hold more than one idea at a time. Just now it's the display she can make with her insurance money. They insure each other and everything insurable, and go half naked in order to do so. The system is perfectly dreadful, but no one can stop them. Probably every man and woman on the place knows exactly what she will receive and half a dozen will come forward with money to lend her, sure of being paid back by this insurance company. It all makes me positively sick, but there is no use trying to control them in that direction. I don't wonder Daddy Neil often says they were better off in the old days when a master looked after their well-being."

An hour later Minervy was driving into Annapolis, three of her boon companions going with her, the "widderless orphans" being left to get on as best they could. She spent the entire morning in town, returning about three o'clock with a wagonful of purchases. Poor Joshua's remains were being looked after by the Society and would later come to Severndale.

Mrs. Harold and the girls were sitting in the charming living-room when Jerome came to ask if Miss Peggy would speak with Minervy a moment.

"Oh, DO bring her in here," begged Mrs. Harold.

Peggy looked doubtful, but consented, and Jerome went to fetch the widow.

When she entered the room Mrs. Harold and the girls were sorely put to it to keep sober faces, for Minervy had certainly outdone herself; not only Minervy, but her entire brood which followed silently and sheepishly behind her. Can Minervy's "mourning" be described? Upon her head rested a huge felt hat of the "Merry Widow" order, and encircling it was a veil of some sort of stiff material, more like crinoline than crape. There were YARDS of it, and so stiff that it stuck straight out behind her like a horse's tail. Under the brim was a white WIDOW'S ruche. Her waist was a black silk one adorned with cheap embroidery, and a broad belt displayed a silver buckle at least four inches in diameter, ornamented with a huge glass carbuncle at least half the buckle's size. On her own huge feet were a pair of shining patent-leather shoes sporting big gilt buckles, and each child wore PATENT-LEATHER DANCING POMPS.

"Why, Minervy," cried Peggy, really distressed, "How COULD you?"

"Why'm, ain' we jist right? I thought I done got bargains wha' jist nachally mak' dat odder widow 'oman tek a back seat AN' sit down. SHE didn't git no sich style when James up an died," answered Minervy, reproach in her tone and eyes.

"But, Minervy," interposed Mrs. Harold. "That bright red stone in the buckle; how can you consider THAT MOURNING? And your veil shouldn't stick - I mean it ought to hang down properly."

Minervy looked deeply perturbed. Shifting from one patent-leather-shod foot to the other, she answered:

"Well'm, well'm, I dare say you's had more spurrience in dese hyer t'ings 'n I is, but dat ston certain'y did strike ma heart. But ef yo' say 'taint right why, pleas ma'am git a pair o' scissors an' prize it out, tho' I done brought de belt fer de sake ob dat buckle. Well, nemmine. I reckons I kin keep it, an' if I ever marhrys agin it sho will come in handy."

The combined efforts of Mrs. Harold, Peggy and Polly eventually got Minervy passably presentable as to raiment, but there they gave up the obligation.

On the following Sunday the funeral was held with all the ceremony and display dear to the African heart, but "Sis Cynthia, Mammy Lucy and Jerome were too occupied with domestic duties to attend." "I holds masef clar 'bove sich goin's-on," was Mammy's dictum. "When *I* dies, I 'spects ter be bur'rid quiet an' dignumfied by ma MISTISS, an' no sich crazy goin's on as dem yonder."

Later Minervy and her "nine haid ob chillern" betook themselves into the town of Annapolis where matrimonial opportunities were greater, and, sure enough, before two months were gone by she presented herself to Peggy, smiling and coy, to ask:

" Please, ma'am, is yo' got any ol' white stuff wha' I

could use fer a bridal veil?"

"A BRIDAL veil?" repeated Peggy, horrified at this new development.

"Yas'm, dat's what I askin' fer. Yo' see, Miss Peggy, dat haid waiter man at de Central Hotel, he done fall in love wid ma nine haid o' po' orphanless chillern an' crave fer ter be a daddy to 'em. An' Miss Peggy, honey, Johanna she gwine be ma bride's maid, an' does yo' reckon yo's got any ole finery what yo' kin giv' her? She's jist 'bout yo' size, ma'am."

Johanna was Minervy's eldest daughter.

"Yes. I'll get exactly what you want," cried Peggy, her lips set and her eyes snapping, for her patience was exhausted.

Going to her storeroom Peggy brought to light about three yards of white cotton net and a pistachio green mull gown, long since discarded. It was made with short white lace sleeves and low cut neck.

"Here you are," she said, handing them to Minervy who was thrown into a state of ecstacy. "But wait a moment; it lacks completeness," and she ran to her room for a huge pink satin bow. "There, tell Johanna to pin THAT on her head and the harlequin ice will be complete."

But her sarcasm missed its mark. Then Peggy went to her greenhouses and gathering a bunch of Killarney roses walked out to the little burial lot where the Severndale help slept and laying them upon Joshua's grave said softly:

"YOU were good and true and faithful, and followed your light."

[Footnote: NOTE - The author would like to state that this episode actually did take place upon the estate of a friend.]

CHAPTER XI

PLAYING GOOD SAMARITAN

February had passed and March was again rushing upon Severndale. A cold, wild March, too. Perhaps because it was coming in like a lion it would go out like a lamb. It is nearly a year since we first saw Peggy Stewart seated in the crotch of the snake-fence talking with Shashai and Tzaritza, and in that year her whole outlook upon life has changed. True it was then later in the month and spring filled the air, but a few weeks make vast changes in a Maryland springtide. And Daddy Neil was coming home soon! Coming in time for an alumni meeting during June week at the Academy, and Mr. Harold was coming also. These facts threw every one at Severndale, as well as Mrs. Harold and Polly into a flutter of anticipation. But several weeks - yes, three whole months in fact - must elapse before they would arrive, for the ships were only just leaving Guantanamo for Hampton Roads and then would follow target practice off the Virginia Capes.

Mrs. Harold and Polly were going to run down to Hampton Roads for a week, to meet Mr. Harold, but Commander Stewart's cruiser would not be there. He was ordered to Nicaragua where one of the periodical insurrections was taking place and Uncle Sam's sailor boys' presence would probably prove salutary. At any rate, Neil Stewart could not be at Hampton Roads, and consequently Peggy decided not to go down with her friends, though urged to join them. Meanwhile she worked away with Compadre and as March slipped by acquired for Severndale a most valuable addition to its paddock.

It all came about in a very simple manner, as such things usually do.

All through Maryland are many small farms, some prosperous, some so slack and forlorn that one wonders how the owners subsist at all. It often depends upon the energy and industry of the individual. These farmers drive into Annapolis with their produce, and when one sees the animals driven, and vehicles to which they are harnessed, one often wonders how the poor beasts have had strength to make the journey even if the vehicle has managed to hold together. Often there is a lively "swapping" of horses at the market-place and a horse may change owners three or four times in the course of a morning.

It so happened that Peggy had driven into Annapolis upon one of these market days, and having driven down to the dock to make inquiry for some delayed freight, was on her way back when she noticed a pair of flea-bitten gray horses harnessed to a ramshackle farm wagon. The wagon wheels were inches thick with dry mud, for the wagon had probably never been washed since it had become its present owner's property. The harness was tied in a dozen places with bits of twine, and the horses were so thin and apparently half-starved that Peggy's heart ached to see them. Pulling up her own span she said to Jess:

"Oh, Jess, how CAN any one treat them so? They seem almost too weak to stand, but they have splendid points. Those horses have seen better days or I'm much mistaken and they come of good stock too."

"Dey sho' does, missie," answered Jess, pleased as Punch to see his young mistress' quick eye for fine horseflesh, though it must be admitted that the fine qualities of these horses were well disguised, and only a connoisseur could have detected them.

As they stood looking at the horses the owner came up accompanied by another man. They were in earnest conversation, the owner evidently protesting and his companion expostulating. Something impelled Peggy to tarry, and without seeming to do so, to listen. She soon grasped the situation: The horses' owner owed the other man some money which he was unable to pay. The argument grew heated. Peggy was unheeded. The upshot was the transfer of ownership of one of the span of horses to the other man, the new owner helping unharness the one chosen, its mate looking on with surprised, questioning eyes, as though asking why he, too, was not being unharnessed. The new owner did not seem over-pleased with his bargain either (he lacked Peggy's discernment) and vented his ill-temper upon the poor horse. Presently he led him away, the mate whinnying and calling after his companion in a manner truly pathetic.

"Quick, Jess," ordered Peggy, "go and find out who that man is and where he is taking that horse, but don't let him suspect why."

Jess scrambled out of the surrey, saying: "Yo' count on ME, Miss Peggy. I's wise, I is; I ketches on all right."

Peggy continued to watch. The man sat down upon an upturned box near his wagon, buried his face in his hands and seemed oblivious of all taking place around him. Presently the horse turned toward him and nickered questioningly. The man looked up and reaching out a work-hardened hand, stroked the poor beast's nose, saying:

"'Taint no use, Pepper; he's done gone fer good. Everythin's gone, and I wisht ter Gawd I was done gone too, fer 'taint no use. The fight's too hard for us."

Just then he caught the eye of the young girl watching him. There was something in her expression which seemed to spell hope: he felt utterly hopeless. She smiled and beckoned to him. She was so used to being obeyed that his response was as a matter of course to her. He moved slowly toward the surrey, resting his hand upon the wheel and looking up at her with listless eyes. "You want me, miss?" he asked.

Peggy said gently:

"I couldn't help seeing what happened; I was right here. Please don't think me inquisitive, but would you mind telling me something about your horses? I love them so, and - and - and - I think yours have good blood."

The furrowed, weatherbeaten face seemed transformed as he answered:

"Some of the best in the land, miss. Some of the best. How did ye guess it?"

"I did not guess it; I knew it. I raise horses."

"Then you're Miss Stewart from Severndale, ain't ye?"

"Yes, and you?"

"I'm jist Jim Bolivar. I live 'bout five mile this side of Severndale. Lived there nigh on ter twenty year, but YO' wouldn't never know me, o' course, though I sometimes drives over to yo' place."

"But how do you expect to drive back all that distance with only one horse? Did you sell the other, or only lend him?"

For a moment the man hesitated. Then looking into the clear, tender eyes he said:

"He had ter go, miss. Everything's gone ag'in me for over a year; I owed Steinberger fifty dollars; I couldn't pay him; I'd given Salt fer s'curity."

"Salt?" repeated Peggy in perplexity.

"Yes'm, Pepper's mate. I named 'em Pepper 'n Salt when they was young colts," and a faint smile curved the speaker's lips. Peggy nodded and said:

"Oh, I see. That was clever. They DO look like pepper and salt."

"Did," corrected the man. "There ain't but one now. But Salt were worth more 'n fifty dollars; yes, he were."

"He certainly was," acquiesced Peggy. "Do you want to sell Pepper too?"

"I'd sell my HEART, miss, if I could get things fer Nell."

"Who is Nell?"

"My girl, miss. Nigh 'bout yo' age, I reckons, but not big an' healthy an' spry like yo'. She's ailin' most o' the time, but we's mighty po,' miss, mighty po'. We ain't allers been, but things have gone agin us pretty steady. Last year the hail spoilt the crops, an' oh well, yo' don't want ter hear 'bout my troubles."

"I want to hear about any one's troubles if I can help them. How shall you get back to your place?"

"Reckon I'll have ter onhitch an' ride Pepper back, on'y I jist natchelly hate ter see Nell's face when I get thar 'thout Salt. She set sich store by them horses, an' they'd foiler her anywheres. I sort ter hate ter start, miss."

"Listen to me," said Peggy. "What does Nell most need?"

"Huh! MOST need? Most need? Well if I started in fer ter tell what she MOST needs I reckon you'd be scart nigh ter death. She needs everythin' an' seems like I can't git nothin'."

"Well what did you hope to get for her?" asked Peggy, making a random shot.

"Why she needs some shoes pretty bad, an' the doctor said she ought ter have nourishin' things ter eat, but, somehow, we can't seem ter git many extras."

" Will you go into the market and get what you'd like

from Mr. Bodwell? Here, give him this and tell him Miss Stewart sent you," and hastily taking a card from her case, Peggy wrote upon it:

"Please give bearer what is needed," and signed her name. "Get a good thick steak and anything else Nell would like."

The man hesitated. "But I ain't askin' charity, miss."

"This is for NELL, and maybe I'll buy Pepper - if SHE will sell him," flashed Peggy, with a radiant smile.

"I'll do as yo' tell me, miss. Mebbe it's Providence. Nell always says: 'The good Lord'll tell us how, Dad,' an' mebbe she's right, mebbe she is," and worn, weary, discouraged Jim Bolivar went toward the market. During his absence Jess returned.

"Dat man's a no' 'count dead beat, Miss Peggy. Yas'm, he is fer a fac', an' he gwine treat dat hawse scan'lous."

Peggy's eyes grew dark. "We'll see," was all she said, but Jess chuckled. Most of the help at Severndale knew that look. "Jess, unharness that horse and tie him behind the surrey," was her next astonishing order.

"Fo' de Lawd's sake, Miss Peggy, what yo' bown' fer ter do? Yo' gwine start hawsestealin'?" Jess didn't know whether to laugh or take it seriously. When Jim Bolivar returned Pepper was trying to reason out the wherefor of being hitched behind such a handsome vehicle as Peggy's surrey, and Jess was protesting:

"But - but - butter," stammered Jess, "Miss Peggy, yo' am' never in de roun' worl' gwine ter drive from de town an' clar out ter Severndale wid dat disrep'u'ble ol' hawse towin' 'long behime WE ALL?"

"I certainly am, and what is more, Jim Bolivar is going to sit on the back seat and hold the leader. He has got to get HOME and he can't without help. Mr. Bolivar, please do as I say," Peggy's voice held a merry note but her little nod of authority meant "business."

"But look at me, miss," protested Bolivar. "I ain't fit ter ride with yo', no how."

"I am not afraid of criticism," replied Peggy, with the little up-tilting of the head which told of her Stewart ancestry. "When I know a thing is right I DO it. Steady, Comet. Quiet, Meteor," for the horses had been standing some time and seemed inclined to proceed upon two legs instead of four. "We'll stop at Brooks' for the shoes, then we'll go around to Dove's; I've a little commission for him."

"Yas'm, yas'm," nodded Jess.

The shoes were bought, Peggy selecting them and giving them to Bolivar with the words: "It will soon be Easter and this is my Easter gift to Nellie, with my love," she added with a smile which made the shoes a hundred-fold more valuable.

Then off to the livery stable.

"Mr. Dove, do you know a man named Steinberger?"

"I know an old skinflint by that name," corrected Dove.

"Well, you are to buy a horse from him. Seventy-five dollars OUGHT to be the price, but a hundred is available if necessary. But do your best. The horse's name is Salt - yes - that is right," as Dove looked incredulous, "and he is a flea-bitten gray - mate to this one behind us. Steinberger bought him today, and I want you to beat him at his own game if you can, for he has certainly beaten a better man."

"You count on me, Miss Stewart, you count on me. Whatever YOU say goes with me."

"Thank you, I'll wait and see what happens."

Their homeward progress was slower than usual, for poor half-starved Pepper could not keep pace with Comet and Meteor. About four miles from Annapolis Bolivar directed them into a by-road which led to an isolated farm, as poor, forlorn a specimen as one could find. But in spite of its disrepair there was something of home in its atmosphere and the dooryard was carefully brushed. Turkey red curtains at the lower windows gave an air of cheeriness to the lonely place. As they drew near a hound came bounding out to greet them with a deep-throated bark, and a moment later a girl about Peggy's age appeared at the door. Peggy thought she had never seen a sweeter or a sadder face. She was fair to transparency with great questioning blue eyes, masses of golden hair waving softly back from her face and gathered into a thick braid. She walked with a slight limp, and looked in surprise at the strange visitors, and her big blue eyes were full of a vague doubt.

"It's all right, honey. It's all right," called Bolivar. "'Aint nothin' but Providence a-workin' out, I reckon, jist like yo' say.

"We have brought your father and Pepper home. Salt is all right, Nelly. You will see him again pretty soon."

"Oh, has anything happened to Salt, Dad?" asked the girl quickly.

"Well, not anything, so-to-speak. Jist let Miss Stewart, here, run it and it'll come out all right. I'm bankin' on that, judgin' from the way she's done so far. She's got a head a mile long, honey, she has, an' has mine beat ter a frazzle. Mine's kind o' wore out I reckon, an' no 'count, no more. Come long out an' say howdy."

Nelly Bolivar came to the surrey and smiling up into Peggy's face, said:

"Of course I know who you are, everybody does, but I never expected to really, truly know you, and I'm a right proud girl to shake hands with you," and a thin hand, showing marks of toil, was held to Peggy. There was a sweet dignity in the act and words.

Peggy took it in her gloved one, saying:

"I didn't suspect I was so well known. For a quiet girl I'm beginning to know a lot of people. But I must go now, it is getting very late. Your father is going to bring Pepper over to see me soon and maybe he will bring you, too. He has such a lot to tell you that I'll not delay it a bit longer. Good-bye, and remember a lot of pleasant things are going to happen," and with the smile which won all who knew her, Peggy drove away.

If people's right ears burn when others are speaking

kindly of them, Peggy's should have burned hard that evening, for Nelly Bolivar listened eagerly as her father told of the afternoon's experiences and Peggy's part in them.

Two days later Salt was delivered at Severndale. Dove had been as good as his word. Shelby gave him one glance and said:

"Well, if some men knew a HOSS as quick as that thar girl does, there'd be fewer no 'count beasts in the world. Put him in a stall and tell Jim Jarvis I want him to take care of him as if he was the Emperor. I know what I'm sayin', an' Miss Peggy knows what she's a-doin', an' that's more 'n I kin say for MOST women-folks."

So Salt found himself in the lap of luxury and one week of it so transformed him that at the end of it poor Pepper would hardly have known his mate. Yet with all the care bestowed upon him the poor horse grieved for his mate, and never did hoof-beat fall upon the ground without his questioning neigh.

Peggy visited him every day and was touched by his response to her petting; it showed what Nelly had done for him. But she was quick to understand the poor creature's nervous watching for his lost mate, and evident loneliness. At length she had him turned into the paddock with the other horses, but even this failed to console him. He stood at the paling looking down the road, again and again neighing his call for the companion which failed to answer. Peggy began to wonder what had become of Jim Bolivar. Two more weeks passed. Mrs. Harold and Polly had returned from Old Point and upon a beautiful April afternoon

Polly and Peggy were out on the little training track where Polly, mounted upon Silver Star, was taking her first lesson in hurdles; a branch of her equestrian education which thus far had not been taken up.

Star was beautifully trained, and took the low hurdles like a lapwing, though it must be confessed that Polly felt as though her head had snapped off short the first time he rose and landed.

"My gracious, Peggy, do you nearly break your neck every time you take a fence?" she cried, settling her hat which had flopped down over her face.

"Not quite," laughed Peggy, skimming over a five-barred hurdle as though it were five inches. "But, oh, Polly, look at Salt! Look at him! He acts as though he'd gone crazy," she cried, for the horse had come to the fence which divided his field from the track and was neighing and pawing in the most excited manner, now and again making feints of springing over.

"Why I believe he would jump if he only knew how," answered Polly eagerly.

"And I believe he DOES know how already," and Peggy slipped from Shashai to go to the fence. Just then, however, the sound of an approaching vehicle caught her ears, and the next instant Salt was tearing away across the field like a wild thing, neighing loudly with every bound, and from the roadway came the answering neigh for which he had waited so long, and Pepper came plodding along, striving his best to hasten toward the call he knew and loved. But Pepper had not been full-fed with oats, corn and bran-mashes, doctored by a skilled hand, or groomed by Jim Jarvis, as Salt had been for nearly four blissful weeks, and an empty stomach is a poor spur. But he could come to the fence and rub noses with Salt, and Peggy and Polly nearly fell into each other's arms with delight.

"Oh, doesn't it make you just want to cry to see them?" said Polly, half tearfully.

"They shan't be separated again," was Peggy's positive assertion. "How do you do, Mr. Bolivar? Why, Nelly, have you been ill?" for the girl looked almost too sick to sit up.

"Yes, Miss Peggy, that's why Dad couldn't come sooner. He had to take care of me. He has fretted terribly over it too, because - "

"Now, now! Tut, tut, honey. Never mind, Miss Peggy don't want to hear nothin' 'bout - "

"Yes she does, too, and Nelly will tell us, She is coming right up to the house with us - this is my friend Miss Polly Howland, Nelly - Nelly Bolivar, Polly - and while you go find Shelby, Mr. Bolivar, and tell him I say to take - oh, here you are, Shelby. This is Mr. Bolivar. Please take him up to your cottage and take GOOD care of him, and give Pepper the very best feed he ever had. Then turn him out in the pasture with Salt. "We will be back again in an hour to talk horse just as fast as we can, and DON'T FORGET WHAT I TOLD YOU ABOUT PEPPER'S POINTS."

"I won't, Miss Peggy, but I ain't got to open more'n HALF an eye no how."

Peggy laughed , then slipping her arm through

Nelly's, said:

"Come up to the house with us. Mammy will know what you need to make you feel stronger, and you are going to be Polly's and my girl this afternoon."

Quick to understand, Polly slipped to Nelly's other side, and the two strong, robust girls, upon whom fortune and Nature had smiled so kindly, led their less fortunate little sister to the great house.

CHAPTER XII

THE SPICE OF PEPPER AND SALT

About an hour later the girls were back at the paddock, Nelly's face alight with joy, for it had not taken good old Mammy long to see that the chief cause of Nelly's lack of strength was lack of proper nourishment, and her skilled old hands were soon busy with sherry and raw eggs as a preliminary, to be followed by one of Aunt Cynthia's dainty little luncheons; a luncheon composed of what Mammy hinted "mus' be somethin' wha' gwine fer ter stick ter dat po' chile's ribs, 'case she jist nachelly half-starved."

Consequently, the half-hour spent in partaking of it did more to put new life in little Nelly Bolivar than many days had done before, and there was physical strength and mental spirit also to sustain her.

The old carryall still stood near the training track and saying:

"Now you sit in there and rest while Polly and I do stunts for your amusement," Peggy helped Nelly into the seat.

"I feel just like a real company lady," said Nelly happily, as she settled herself to watch the girls whom she admired with all the ardor of her starved little soul.

"You ARE a real company lady," answered Peggy and Polly, "and we are going to entertain you with a sure-enough circus. All you've got to do is to applaud vigorously no matter how poor the show. Come on, Polly," and springing upon their horses, which had mean-time been patiently waiting in the care of Bud, off they raced around the track, Nelly watching with fascinated gaze.

Meanwhile Pepper and Salt had been rejoicing in their reunion, Salt full of spirit and pranks as the result of his good care, and poor Pepper, for once full-fed, wonderfully "chirkered" up in consequence, though in sharp contrast to his mate.

As Peggy and Polly cavorted around the track, racing, jumping and cutting all manner of pranks, Salt's attention to his mate seemed to be diverted. The antics of Star and Shashai, unhampered, happy and free as wild things, seemed to excite him past control. Again and again he ran snorting toward the paling, turning to whinny an invitation to Pepper, but, even with his poor, half-starved stomach for once well-filled, Pepper could not enthuse as his mate did; ONE square meal a year cannot compensate for so many others missed, and bring about miracles.

Around and around the track swept the girls, taking hurdles, and cutting a dozen antics. At length Peggy, who had been watching Salt, stopped, and saying to Polly:

"I'm going to try an experiment," she slipped from Shashai's back. Going to the fence she vaulted the four-foot barrier as easily as Shashai would have skimmed over six. Salt came to her at once, but Pepper hesitated. It was only momentary, for soon both heads were nestling confidingly to her. She was never without her little bag of sugar and a lump or two were eagerly accepted. Then going to Salt's side she crooned into his ear some of her mysterious "nightmare talk," as Shelby called it. It was a curious power the girl exercised over animals - almost hypnotic. Salt nozzled and fussed over her. Then saying:

"Steady, boy. Steady." She gave one of her sudden springs and landed astride his back, saddleless and halterless. He gave a startled snort and tore away around the paddock. Polly was now used to any new departure, but Nelly gave a little shriek and clasped her hands. "She is all right, don't be frightened," smiled Polly. "She can do anything with a horse; I sometimes think she must have been a horse herself once upon a time." Nelly looked puzzled, but Polly laughed. Meanwhile Peggy was talking to her unusual mount. He seemed a trifle bewildered, but presently struck into a long, sweeping run - the perfect stride of the racer. Peggy gave a quick little nod of understanding as she felt the long, gliding motion she knew so well. As she came around to her friends she reached forward and laying hold of a strand of the silvery mane, said softly: "Who - ooa. Steady." What was it in the girl's voice which commanded obedience? Salt stopped close to his mate and began to rub noses with him as though confiding a secret.

"Bud," commanded Peggy, "go to the stable and fetch me a snaffle bridle." The bridle was brought and carefully adjusted.

"Come, Salt, NOW we will put it to the test; those flank muscles mean something unless I'm mistaken."

During all this Shelby and Bolivar had come up to the paddock and stood watching the girl.

"Ain't she jist one fair clipper?" asked Shelby, proudly. "Lord, but that girl's worth about a dozen of your ornery kind. She's a thoroughbred all through, she is."

"Well, I ain't never seen nothin' like that, fer a fact, I ain't. I knowed them was good horses, but, well, I didn't know they was SADDLE horses."

"They've more'n SADDLE horses, man, an' I'm bettin' a month's wages your eyes'll fair pop out inside five minutes. I know HER ways. I larned 'em to her, some on 'em, at least - but most was born in her. They HAS ter be. There's some things can't be L'ARNT, man."

Once more Peggy started, this time her mount showing greater confidence in her. At first they loped lightly around the paddock, poor old Pepper alternately following, then stopping to look at his mate, apparently trying to reason it all out. Gradually the pace increased until once more Salt swept along in the stride which from time immemorial has distinguished racing blood. The fifth time around the broad field, Peggy turned him suddenly and making straight for the paling, cried in a ringing voice:

"On! On! Up - Over!"

The horse quivered, his muscles grew tense, then there was a gathering together of the best in him and the fence was taken as only running blood takes an obstacle.

Then HER surprise came:

Pepper meantime seemed to have lost his wits. As Salt
neared the fence, the mate who for years had plodded
beside him began to tear around and around the field,
snorting, whinnying and giving way to the wildest
excitement. As Salt skimmed over the fence Pepper's
decorum fled, and with a loud neigh he tore after him,
made a wild leap and cleared the barrier by a foot, then
startled and shaken from his unwonted exertion, he
stood with legs wide apart, trembling and quivering.

In an instant Peggy had wheeled her mount and was
beside the poor frightened creature; frightened because
his blood had asserted itself and he had literally
outdone himself. Slipping from Salt's back she tossed
her bridle to Shelby who had hurried toward her, and
taking Pepper's head in her arms petted and caressed
him as she would have petted and caressed a child
which had made a superhuman effort to perform some
seemingly impossible act.

"Nelly, Nelly, come here. Come. He will know your
voice so much better than mine," she called, and Nelly
scrambled out of the wagon as quickly as possible,
crying:

"Why, Miss Stewart, HOW did you do it. Why we
never knew they were so wonderful. Oh, Dad, did you
know they could jump and run like that?"

"I knew they come o' stock that HAD run, an' jumped
like that, but I didn't know all that ginger was in 'em.
No I did NOT. It took Miss Stewart fer ter find THAT

out, an' she sure has found it. Why, Pepper, old hoss," he added, stroking the horse's neck, "you've sartin' done yo'self proud this day."

Pepper nozzled and nickered over him, evidently trying to tell him that the act had been partly inspired by the call of the blood, and partly by his love for his mate. Perhaps Bolivar did not interpret it just that way, but PEGGY DID.

"Mr. Bolivar, I know Nelly loves Pepper and Salt, but I'd like to make you an offer for those horses just the same. I knew when I first saw them that they had splendid possibilities and only needed half a chance. You need two strong, able work-horses for your farm - these horses are both too high-bred for such work, that you know as well as I do - so I propose that we make a sensible bargain right now. We have a span of bays; good, stout fellows six years old, which we have used on the estate. They shall be yours for this pair with one hundred and twenty-five dollars to boot. Salt and Pepper are worth six hundred dollars right now, and in a little while, and under proper care and training, will be worth a good deal more. Shelby will bear me out in that, won't you?"

"I'd be a plumb fool if I didn't, miss," was Shelby's reply, and Peggy nodded and resumed: "I have paid seventy-five dollars for Salt, adding to that the one-twenty-five and the span, which I value at four hundred, would make it a square deal, don't you think so?"

Bolivar looked at the girl as though he thought she had taken leave of her wits. "One hundred and twenty-five dollars, and a span worth four hundred for a pair of horses which a month before he would have found it hard to sell for seventy-five each? - well, Miss Stewart must certainly be crazy." Peggy laughed at his bewilderment.

"I'm perfectly serious, Mr. Bolivar," she said.

"Yas'm, yas'm, but, my Lord, miss, I ain't seen THAT much money in two year, and your horses - I ain't seen 'em, and I don't want ter; if YOU say they're worth it that goes, but - but - well, well, things has been sort o' tough - sort o' tough," and poor, tired, discouraged Jim Bolivar leaned upon the fence and wept from sheer bodily weakness and nervous exhaustion.

Nelly ran to his side to clasp her arms about him and cry:

"Dad! Dad! Poor Dad. Don't! Don't! It's all right, Dad. We won't worry about things. God has taken care of us so far and He isn't going to stop."

"That ain't it, honey. That ain't it," said poor Bolivar, slipping a trembling arm about her. "It's - it's - oh, I can't jist rightly say what 'tis."

"Wall by all that's great, *I* know, then," exclaimed Shelby, clapping him on the shoulder. "*I* know, 'cause I've BEEN there: It's bein' jist down, out an' discouraged with everythin' and not a blame soul fer ter give a man a boost when he needs it. I lived all through that kind o' thing afore I came ter Severndale, an' 'taint a picter I like fer ter dwell upon. No it ain't, an' we're goin' ter bust yours ter smithereens right now. You don't want fer ter look at it no longer."

"No I don't, I don't fer a fact," answered Bolivar, striving manfully to pull himself together and dashing from his eyes the tears which he felt had disgraced him.

Peggy drew near. Her eyes were soft and tender as a doe's, and the pretty lips quivered as she said:

"Mr. Bolivar, please don't try to go home tonight. Shelby can put you up, and Nelly shall stay with me. You are tired and worn out and the change will do you good. Then you can see the horses and talk it all over with Shelby, and by tomorrow things will look a lot brighter. And Nelly and I will have a little talk together too."

"I can't thank ye, miss. No, I can't. There ain't no words big nor grand enough fer ter do that. I ain't never seen nothin' like it, an' yo've made a kind o' heaven fer Nelly. Yes, go 'long with Miss Peggy, honey. Ye ain't never been so looked after since yo' ma went on ter Kingdom Come." He kissed the delicate little face and turning to Shelby, said:

"Now come on an' I'll quit actin' like a fool."

"There's other kinds o' fools in this world," was Shelby's cryptic reply. "Jim," he called, "look after them horses," indicating Pepper and Salt, and once more united, the two were led away to the big stable where their future was destined to bring fame to Severndale.

Bolivar went with Shelby to his quarters, and their interest in riding having given way to the greater one in Nelly, the girls told Bud to take their horses back to the stable. From that moment, Nelly Bolivar's life was transformed. The following day she and her father went back to the little farm behind the well conditioned span from Severndale, and a good supply of provisions for all, for Shelby had insisted upon giving them what he called, "a good send off" on his own account, and enough oats and corn went with Tom and Jerry, as the new horses were named, to keep them well provisioned for many a day.

"Jist give 'em half a show an' they'll earn their keep," advised Shelby. "I'll stop over before long and lend a hand gettin' things ship-shape. I know they're boun' ter get out o' kilter when yo' don't have anybody ter help. One pair o' hands kin only do jist so much no matter how hard they work. Good luck."

From that hour Nelly was Peggy's protege. The little motherless girl living so close to Severndale, her home, her circumstances in such contrast to her own, wakened in Peggy an understanding of what lay almost at her door, and so many trips were made to the little farm-house that spring that Shashai and Tzaritza often started in that direction of their own accord when Peggy set forth upon one of her outings.

And meanwhile, over in the hospital, Dunmore was growing weaker and weaker as the advancing springtide was bringing to Nelly Bolivar renewed health and strength, so strangely are things ordered in this world, and with Easter the brave spirit took its flight, leaving many to mourn the lad whom all had so loved. For some time the shadow of his passing lay upon the Academy, then spring athletics absorbed every one's interest and Ralph made the crew, to Polly's intense delight. In May he rowed on the plebe crew against a high school crew and beat them "to a standstill." Then came rehearsal for the show to be given by the Masqueraders, the midshipmen's dramatic association, and at this occurred something which would have been pronounced utterly impossible had the world's opinion been asked. The show was to be given the last week in May.

Mr. Harold and Mr. Stewart would arrive a few days before, each on a month's leave. As Happy was one of the moving spirits of the show, he was up to his eyes in business. Clever in everything he undertook, he was especially talented in music, playing well and composing in no mediocre manner. He had written practically all the score of the musical comedy to be given by the Masqueraders, and among other features, a whistling chorus.

Now if there was one thing Polly could do it was whistle. Indeed, she insisted that it was her only accomplishment and many a happy little impromptu concert was given in Middies' Haven with Happy's guitar, Shortie's mandolin and Durand's violin.

Of course, all the characters in the play were taken by the boys, many of them making perfectly fascinating girls, but when the whistling chorus was written by Happy, Polly was no small aid to him, and again and again this chorus was rehearsed in Middies' Haven, sometimes by a few of the number who would compose it, and again by the entire number; the star performer being a little chap from Ralph's class whose voice still held its boyish treble and whose whistle was like a bird's notes. Naturally, Polly had learned the entire score, for one afternoon during the past autumn while the girls were riding through the beautiful woodlands near Severndale, Polly had whistled an answer to a bob-white's call. So perfect had been her mimicry that the bird had been completely deceived and answering repeatedly, had walked almost up to Silver Star's feet. Peggy was enraptured, and then learned that Polly could mimic many bird calls, and whistle as sweetly as the birds themselves. Peggy had lost no time in making this known to the boys, much to Polly's embarrassment, but the outcome had been the delightful little concerts, and Happy had made the various bird notes the theme of his bird chorus. It was a wonderfully pretty thing and bound to make a big hit, so all agreed. Consequently, little Van Nostrand had been drilled until he declared he woke himself up in the night whistling, and so the days sped away. Mr. Harold and Daddy Neil had arrived and the morning of the Masqueraders' show dawned. In less than twelve hours the bird chorus would be on the stage whistling Polly's bird notes. Then Wharton Van Nostrand fell ill with tonsilitis and was packed off to the hospital!

Happy was desperate. Who under the sun would take his part? There was not another man whose voice was like Wharton's. Happy flew about like a distracted hen, at length rushing to Mrs. Harold and begging her to give him just TEN minutes private interview.

"Why, what under the sun do you want, Happy?" she asked, going into her own room and debarring all the others whose curiosity was at the snapping point. When they emerged Happy's face was brimful of glee, but Mrs. Harold warned:

"Mind the promise is only conditional: If Polly says 'yes' well and good, but if you let the secret out you and I will be enemies forevermore."

CHAPTER XIII

THE MASQUERADERS' SHOW

It was the night of the Masqueraders' Show. The auditorium was packed, for Annapolis was thronged with the relatives of the graduating class as well as hundreds of visitors.

Among others were Polly Howland's mother, her married sister Constance, and her brother-in-law, Harry Hunter, now an ensign. They had been married at Polly's home in Montgentian, N.J., almost a year ago. Harry Hunter had graduated from the Academy the year Happy and his class were plebes, and had been the two-striper of the company of which Wheedles was now the two-striper. His return to Annapolis with his lovely young wife was the signal for all manner of festive doings, and it need hardly be added that Mrs. Harold's party had a row of seats which commanded every corner of the stage. Mr. Stewart and Peggy were of the party, of course, and anything radiating more perfect happiness than Peggy's face that night it would have been hard to find. Was not Daddy Neil beside her, and in her private opinion the finest looking officer present? Again and again as she sat next him she slipped her hand into his to give it a rapturous little squeeze. Nor was "Daddy Neil" lacking in appreciation of the favors of the gods. The young girl sitting at his side, in spite of her modesty and utter lack of self-consciousness, was quite charming enough to make any parent's heart thrill with pride. With her exceptional tact, Mrs. Harold had won Harrison's favor, Harrison pronouncing her: "A real, born lady, more like your own ma than any one you've met up with since you lost her; SHE was one perfect lady if one ever lived."

It had been rather a delicate position for Mrs. Harold to assume, that of unauthorized guardian and counsellor to this young girl who had come into her life by such an odd chance, but Mrs. Harold seemed to be born to mother all the world, and subtly Harrison recognized the fact that Peggy was growing beyond her care and guidance, and the thousand little amenities of the social world in which she would so soon move and have her being. For more than a year this knowledge had been a source of disquietude to the good soul who for eight years had guarded her little charge so faithfully, and she had often confided to Mammy Lucy:

"That child is getting clear beyond ME. She's growin' up that fast it fair takes my breath away, and she knows more right now in five minutes than I ever knew in my whole life, though 'twouldn't never in this world do to let her suspicion it."

Consequently, once having sized up Mrs. Harold, and fully decided as the months rolled by that she "weren't no meddlesome busybody, a-trying to run things," she was only too glad to ask her advice in many instances, and Peggy's toilet this evening was one of them. Poor old Harrison had begun to find the intricacies of a young girl's toilet a trifle too complex for her, and had gone to Mrs. Harold for advice. The manner in which it was given removed any lingering vestige of doubt remaining in Harrison's soul, and tonight Peggy was a vision of girlish loveliness in a soft pink crepe meteor made with a baby waist, the round neck frilled with the softest lace, the little puffed sleeves edged with it, and a "Madam Butterfly" sash and bow of the crepe encircling her lithe waist. Her hair was drawn loosely back and tied a la pompadour with a bow of pink satin ribbon, another gathering in the rich, soft abundance of it just below the neck.

By chance she sat between Mrs. Howland and her father, Mrs. Harold was next Mrs. Howland, with Mr. Harold, Constance and Snap just beyond, and Polly at the very end of the seat, though why she had slipped there Mrs. Howland could not understand.

Peggy had instantly been attracted to Mrs. Howland and had fallen in love with Constance as only a young girl can give way to her admiration for another several years her senior. But there was nothing of the foolish "crush" in her attitude: it was the wholesome admiration of a normal girl, and Constance was quick to feel it. Mrs. Howland was smaller and daintier than Mrs. Harold, though in other ways there was a striking resemblance between these two sisters. Mrs. Harold, largely as the result of having lived among people in the service, was prompt, decisive of action, and rather commanding in manner, though possessing a most tender, sympathetic heart. Mrs. Howland, whose whole life had been spent in her home, with the exception of the trips taken with her husband and children when they were young, for she had been a widow many years, had a rather retiring manner, gentle and lovable, and, as Peggy thought, altogether adorable, for her manner with Polly was tenderness itself, and Polly's love for her mother was constantly manifested in a thousand little affectionate acts. She had a little trick of running up to her and half crying, half crooning:

"Let me play cooney-kitten and get close," and then nestling her sunny head into her mother's neck, where the darker head invariably snuggled down against it and a caressing hand stroked the spun gold as a gentle voice said:

"Mother's sun-child. The little daughter who helps fill her world with light." Polly loved to hear those words and Peggy thought how dear it must be to have some claim to such a tender love and know that one meant so much to the joy and happiness of another.

Mrs. Harold had written a great deal of Peggy's history to this sister, so Mrs. Howland felt by no means a stranger to the young girl beside her, and her heart was full of sympathy when she thought of her lonely life in spite of all this world had given her of worldly goods.

Meantime the little opera opened with a dashing chorus, a ballet composed, apparently, of about fifty fetching young girls, gowned in the most up-to-date costumes, wearing large picture hats which were the envy of many a real feminine heart in the audience, and carrying green parsols with long sticks and fascinating tassles. Oh, the costumer knew his business and those dainty high-heeled French slippers seemed at least five sizes smaller than they really were as they tripped so lightly through the mazes of the ballet. But alack! the illusion was just a TRIFLE dispelled when the ballet-girls broke into a rollicking chorus, for some of those voices boomed across the auditorium with an undoubtable masculine power.

Nevertheless, the ballet was encored until the poor dancers were mopping rouge-tinged perspiration from their faces. One scene followed another in rapid order, all going off without a hitch until the curtain fell upon the first act, and during the interval and general bustle of friend greeting friend Polly and Mrs. Harold disappeared. At first, Mrs. Howland was not aware of their absence, then becoming alive to it she asked:

"Connie, dear, what has become of Aunt Janet and Polly?"

"I am sure I don't know, mother. They were here only a moment ago," answered Constance.

"I saw them go off with Happy, beating it for all they were worth toward the wings, Carissima," answered Snap, using for Mrs. Howland the name he had given her when he first met her, for this splendid big son-in-law loved her as though she were his own mother, and that love was returned in full.

"Peggy, dear, can you enlighten us?" asked Mrs. Howland looking at the girl beside her, for her lips were twitching and her eyes a-twinkle.

Peggy laughed outright, then cried contritely:

"Oh, I beg your pardon, Mrs. Howland, I did not mean to be rude, but it is a secret, and such a funny one, too; I'd tell if I dared but I've promised not to breathe it."

"Run out an extra cable then, daughter," laughed Commander Stewart.

" I think this one will hold , " was Mrs. Howland's

prompt answer, with a little pat upon Peggy's soft arm. "She's a staunch little craft, I fancy. I won't ask a single question if I must not." A moment later the lights were lowered and the curtains were rung back. The scene drew instant applause. It was a pretty woodland with a stream flowing in the background. Grouped upon the stage in picturesque attitudes were about forty figures costumed to represent various birds, and in their midst was a charming little maiden, evidently the only human being in this bird-world, and presently it was disclosed to the audience that she was held as a hostage to these bird-beings, until the prince of their enchanted world should be released from bondage in the land of human beings and restored to them.

"Why who in this world can that little chap be?"

"I didn't know there was such a tiny midshipman in the whole brigade."

"Doesn't he make a perfectly darling girl, though?"

"Perfectly lovable, hugable and adorable," were the laughing comments.

In the dim light Peggy buried her head in Daddy Neil's lap, trying to smother her laughter.

"You - you little conspirator," he whispered. "I believe I've caught on."

"Oh, don't whisper it. Don't!" instantly begged Peggy. "Polly would never forgive me for letting out the secret."

" You haven't. I just did a little Yankee guessing, and I

reckon I'm not far from the mark."

"Hush, and listen. Isn't it pretty?"

It was, indeed, pretty. The captive princess, captured because she had learned the secret of the bird language, began a little plaintive whistling call, soft, sweet, musical as a flute; the perfect notes of the hermit thrush. This was evidently the theme to be elaborated upon and the chorus took it up, led so easily, so harmoniously and so faultlessly by the dainty little figure with its bird-like notes. From the hermit-thrush's note to the liquid call of the wood-thrush, the wood-peewee, the cardinal's cheery song, the whip-poor-will's insistent questioning, on through the gamut of cat-birds, warblers, bob-whites and a dozen others, ran the pretty chorus, with its variations, the little princess' and her jailor birds' dancing and whistling completing the clever theme. When it ended the house went mad clapping, calling, shouting: "Encore! Encore!"

And before it could be satisfied the obliging actors had given their chorus and ballet five times, and the whistlers' throats were dry as powder. As they left the stage for the last time the little princess flung HERself into Mrs. Harold's arms, gasping.

"I know my whistle is smashed, destroyed, and mined beyond repair, Aunt Janet, but oh, wasn't it perfectly splendid to do it for the boys and hear that house applaud them."

"Them?" cried a feathered creature coming up to give Polly a clap upon the back as he would have given a classmate. "Them! And where the mischief do YOU come in on this show-down? There listen to that. Do you know what it means? It means come out there in front of that curtain and get what's coming to you. Come on."

"Oh, I can't! I can't! They'd recognize me and I wouldn't have them for worlds. Not for worlds! It would be perfectly awful," and Polly shrank back abashed.

"Recognized! Awful nothing! You've got to come out. It's part of the performance," and hand in hand with Happy and Wheedles the abashed little princess was led before the foot-lights to receive an ovation and enough American beauty roses to hide her in a good-sized bower. As she started back she let fall some of her posies. Instantly, Wheedles was upon his knees, his hand pressed to his heart, and his eyes dancing with fun, as he handed her the roses. Shouts and renewed applause went up from the auditorium.

"I KNOW that is a girl. I am positive of it. But WHO can she be?" was the comment of one of the ladies behind Mrs. Howland.

"Well I have an idea *I* might tell her name if I chose," said Mrs. Howland under her breath to Peggy.

"Didn't she do it beautifully?" whispered Peggy, squeezing Mrs. Howland's hand in a rapture. "But please don't tell. Please don't."

Mrs. Howland smiled down upon the eager face upraised to hers. "Do you think I am likely to?" she asked.

Peggy nodded her head in negative, but before she could say more Polly and another girl came walking down the aisle. Even Peggy looked in surprise at the newcomer, then she gave a little gasp. The girl was much taller than Polly, and rather broad shouldered for a girl, but strange to relate, looked enough like Peggy to be her twin. Mr. Stewart gave a startled exclamation and seemed about to rise from his seat. Peggy laid a detaining hand upon his and whispered: "Don't." Her father looked at her as though he did not know whether his wits or hers were departing. The play was again in progress so Polly and her companion took their seats next Mrs. Harold who had returned some minutes before. Polly was doing her best to control her laughter, but the girl with her was the very personification of decorum.

"In heaven's name who IS that girl?" Peggy's father asked in a low voice.

"He's - he's - " and Peggy broke down.

"What?"

"Yes - I'll tell you later, but isn't it too funny for words?"

"Why child she - he-ahem - that PERSON is enough like you to be your sister. Who - " and poor puzzled Neil Stewart was too bewildered to complete his sentence or follow the play.

"Yes; I've known that from the first and it is perfectly absurd," answered Peggy, "but I never realized HOW like me until this minute. But he will catch the very mischief if he is found out. But WHERE did he get those clothes? They aren't a part of the costumes so far as I know."

But there is just where Peggy's calculations fell down, for the dainty lingerie gown, with its exquisite Charlotte Corday hat had been added to the costumes to substitute others which had been ordered but could not be supplied. Consequently Peggy had not happened to see it.

And the handsome girl? Well she certainly WAS a beauty with her dark hair, perfect eyebrows, flashing dark eyes and faultless teeth. Her skin was dark but the cheeks were mantled with a wonderful color. As the play was still in progress, she could not, of course, enter into conversation with Polly's friends, but her smile was fascinating to a rare degree.

At length the second act ended, and Neil Stewart could stand it no longer.

"Peggy, introduce me to that girl right off. Why - why, she might be you," and Peggy's father fairly mopped his brow in perturbation.

Peggy beckoned to the new arrival who managed to slip around the aisle and come to her end of the seat. If she minced with a rather affected step it was not commented upon. Most people were too fascinated by her beauty to criticise her walk. The look which the two exchanged puzzled Mr. Stewart more than ever. Peggy's lips were quivering as she said:

"Miss - er, Miss Leroux, I want you to know Mrs. Howland and my father."

"So delighted to," replied "Miss" Leroux, but at the words Mrs. Rowland gave a little gasp and Mr. Stewart who had risen to meet Peggy's friend, started as though some one had struck him, for the voice, even with Durand's best attempts to disguise it to a feminine pitch, held a quality which no girl's voice ever held.

"Well I'll be - I'll be - why you unqualified scamp, who ARE you, and what do you mean by looking so exactly like my girl here that I don't know whether I've one daughter or two?" Then Durand fled, laughing as only Durand could - with eyes, lips and an indescribable expression which made both the laugh and himself absolutely irresistible.

The following week sped away and before any one quite knew where it had gone the great June ball was a thing of the past and the morning had come which would mean the dividing of the ways for many.

Happy, Wheedles, and Shortie had graduated and would have a month's leave. Durand was now a second-classman, Ralph a youngster, and about to start upon the summer practice cruise.

The ships were to run down to Hampton Roads and then up to New London, where Mrs. Harold and all her party were to meet them, she and Mrs. Howland having taken rooms at the Griswold for the period the ships would be at New London.

They had asked Peggy to go with them and when "Daddy Neil" arrived he was included in the invitation.

But Daddy Neil had a plan or two of his own, and these plans he was not long in turning over with Mr.

Harold to the satisfaction of all concerned, and they all decided that they "beat the first ones out of sight."

As Daddy Neil was a man of prompt action he was not long in carrying them into effect, and they were nothing more nor less than a big house party in New London rather than the hotel life which had been planned. So telegraph wires were kept busy, and in no time one of the Griswold cottages was at the disposal of the entire party.

CHAPTER XIV

OFF FOR NEW LONDON

"Now I'm going to run THIS show, Harold, and you may just as well pipe down," rumbled Neil Stewart in his deep, wholesome voice. "Besides, I'm your ranking officer and here's where I prove it," he added, forcing Mr. Harold into his pet Morris chair and towering above him, his genial laugh filling the room.

It was the Sunday afternoon following graduation. Many, indeed the greater portion of the graduates, had left for their homes, or to pay visits to friends before joining their ships at the end of their month's leave, though some still lingered, their plans as yet unformed.

Wilmot Hall was practically deserted, for the scattering which takes place after graduation is hard to understand unless one is upon the scene to witness it.

Mr. and Mrs. Harold, with Mr. Stewart, Peggy, Mrs. Howland, Constance, Snap, Polly, Shortie, Wheedles and Happy were gathered in Middies' Haven, and Neil Stewart had the floor. Since his return to Severndale he had spent more than half the time at Wilmot where his lodestar, Peggy, was staying with those she had grown to love so dearly, and where she was so entirely happy. Mr. Stewart had taken a room for June week in order to be near her, feeling reluctant to take her away from the friends who had done so much for her; more, a vast deal, he felt, than he could ever repay. It did not take him long to see the change which nine months had made in this little girl of his.

Always lovable and exceptionally capable, there was now the added charm which association with a girl of her own age had developed in spontaneity, and her attitude toward Mrs. Harold - the pretty little affectionate demonstrations so unconsciously made - revealed to her father what Peggy had lacked for nearly nine years, and he began to waken to the fact to which Mrs. Harold had been alive for some time: that without meaning to be selfish in his sorrow for Peggy's mother, he had been wholly self-absorbed, leaving Peggy to live her life in a little world of her own creation.

During the past two weeks HE had been put through a pretty severe scrutiny by Mrs. Harold, and in spite of her prejudices she began to see how circumstances had conspired to evolve the unusual order of things for both father and daughter, and her heart softened toward the big man who, while so complete a master of every situation on board his own ship, was so helpless to cope with this domestic problem. Nor could she see her way clear to remedy it further than she had already done. It seemed to be one of life's handicaps. But we can not understand the "why" of all things in this world, and must leave a great deal of it to the Father of all. Just now it seemed as though Neil Stewart was the instrument of that ordering.

Mr. Harold looked up at him and joined in the laugh.

" Maybe you think I'm going to give these fellows a

demonstration of insubordination the very first clip. Not on your life. Fire away. You have the deck."

"Well, I've got my cottage up there in New London - a good one too, if I can judge by all the hot air that has escaped concerning it. Jerome and Mammy are packed off to open it up and make it habitable against our arrival, and everything's all skee and shipshape so far as THAT part of the plan is blocked out. The ship's in commission but now comes the question of her personnel. You, Harold, and your wife have been good enough to act as second and third in command but we must have junior officers. Thus far the detail foots up only five; just a trifle shy on numbers, and I want it to number, let me see, at least eleven," and he nodded toward the others seated about the room. Some looked at him in doubt. Then Happy said:

"But, Mr. Stewart. I'm afraid I've got to beat it for home, sir."

"Where is home?"

"Up the Hudson, sir."

"That's all right. And yours?" indicating Shortie.

"Vermont, sir."

"And yours?"

"Near Philadelphia, sir," said Wheedles.

"All within twelve hours of New London, aren't they?"

"Yes sir."

"Very well; that settles it. You give us ten days at least, and we'll do the Regatta at New London and any other old thing worth doing. Will you wire your people that you're going with us? 'Orders from your superior officer.' Who knows but you may all hit my ship and in that case you may as well fall in at once."

"Well you better believe there'll be no kick - I beg your pardon sir - I mean, I'll be delighted," stammered Happy.

"That Western Union wire is going to fuse, sir," was Wheedles' characteristic response.

"I said last time I was up at New London that I'd be singed and sizzled if I ever went again, sir, and that just goes to show 'what fools we mortals be'," was Shortie's quizzical answer.

"Orders received and promptly obeyed. So far so good," was the hearty response. "Now to the next. Mrs. Howland, what about you and your plans! We've got this little girl in tow all tight and fast, but you haven't put out a signal."

"It all sounds most enticing, but do you know I have another girl to think about? She is up at Smith College and will graduate in one week. I must be there for THAT if I never do another thing. It is an event in her life and mine."

"Hum; yes; I see; of course. We've got to get around that, haven't we? And I dare say YOU two think you've got to be on deck also," he added, nodding at Constance and Snap, who in return nodded their reply in a very positive manner.

"Are you going to jump ship too, little captain?" he asked, turning suddenly to Polly.

"Oh please don't. We need you so much," pleaded Peggy.

"I'd like to see Gail graduate, but oh, I do want to go to New London just dreadfully," cried Polly.

"You would better go, dear," said Mrs. Howland, deciding the question for her. "You would have but three days at Northampton and they would hardly mean as much to you as the same number at New London. Constance, Snap and I will go up, and then perhaps we will come on to New London. I must first learn Gail's plans."

"You will ALL come up. Every last one of you, Gail too; and if Gail bears even a passing resemblance to the rest of her family she isn't going to disgrace it."

"She's perfectly lovely, Mr. Stewart," was Polly's emphatic praise of her pretty, twenty-year-old sister.

"Your word goes, captain," answered Mr. Stewart, crossing the room to where the girls sat upon the couch. "Gangway, please," he said, motioning them apart and seating himself between them. "My, but these are pretty snug quarters," he added, placing an arm around each and drawing them close to him. Peggy promptly nestled her head upon his shoulder.

"My other shoulder feels lonesome," said Mr. Stewart, smiling into Polly's face. The next second the bronze head was cuddled down also. "That's pretty nice. Best game of rouge et noir ever invented," nodded Neil

Stewart, a happy smile upon his strong face. "Now to proceed: There are, thus far, eleven of us. When we capture Gail we shall have twelve. A round dozen. Good! Now how to get up there is the next question. I've hit it! Let's make an auto trip of it."

"An auto trip," chorused the others.

"Sure thing! Why not? Look here, people, this is my holiday. Such a holiday as I haven't had in years, and at the end of it is something else for me. Harold knows, but he's been too wise to give it away. I didn't know it myself until I came through Washington, but - well - it's pretty good news. I didn't mean to blurt it out, but this is sort of a family conclave and I needn't ask you all to keep it in the family; but up there in the Boston Navy Yard is an old fighting machine of which I am to be captain when I get back in harness - "

"What! Oh, Daddy! Daddy! How splendid!" cried Peggy. "Oh, I've just got to hug you hard," and she smothered him in a regular bear hug.

"That's better than the promotion," he said, his eyes shining, and his thoughts harking back to another impulsive young girl who had clasped her arms about him when he received his commission as lieutenant. How like her Peggy was growing. It would have meant a good deal to her could she have lived to see him attain his captaincy. He always recalled her as a young girl. It was almost impossible for him to realize that were she now alive she would be Mrs. Harold's age, though she was considerably younger than himself when they had married.

And so it was settled. Neil Stewart was to engage a

couple of large touring cars for a month and in these the party was to make the trip to New London. A man of prompt action, he lost no time in putting his plan into effect, and the following Wednesday a merry party set out from Wilmot Hall. Each car carried six comfortably in addition to the chauffeur.

Each was provided with everything necessary for the long trip which they calculated would take about three days, and the pairing off was arranged to every one's satisfaction, an arrangement known to have exceptions. Mr. and Mrs. Harold, Happy, Shortie and Polly and Peggy were in one car, Mr. Stewart, Mrs. Howland, Snap, Constance and Wheedles in the other, the extra seat, Mr. Stewart said was to be held in reserve for Gail when Mrs. Howland should bring her to New London.

None of the party ever forgot that auto ride through Maryland, Pennsylvania, New Jersey, New York and Connecticut. The weather was ideal, and for the men just ashore after months of sea-duty, and the midshipmen, just emancipated from four years of the strictest discipline and a most limited horizon, it was a most wonderful world of green things, and an endless panorama of beauty.

One night was spent in Philadelphia where all stopped at the Aldine and went to see "The Balkan Princess." Another night in New York at the Astor with "Excuse Me" to throw every one into hysterics of laughter.

And what a revelation it all was to Peggy. What a new world she had entered.

" I didn't know there could be anything like it," she

confided to Polly, "and oh, isn't it splendid. But HOW I wish I could just share it with everybody."

"It seems to me you are sharing it with a good many bodies, Peggy Stewart. What do you call ten people besides yourself?"

"Oh, I mean people who never have or see anything like it. Like Nelly, for instance, and - and - oh just dozens of people who seem to go all their lives and never have any of the things which so many other people have. I wonder why it IS so, Polly? It doesn't seem just right, does it?"

"I wonder if you know how many people you make happy in the course of a year, Peggy Stewart. I don't believe you have the least idea, but it's a pity a few of them couldn't lift up their voices and make it known."

"Well, I'm right thankful they can't. It would be awful."

It was a glorious June afternoon when the two big touring cars swept under the porte-cochere of the Griswold Hotel at New London, and attendants hurried out to assist the new arrivals from them. Mr. Stewart waved them aside and saying to his guests:

"Wait here until I find out where that shack of ours is located and then we'll go right over to it and get fixed tip as soon as possible," he disappeared into the hotel to return a moment later with a clerk.

"This man will direct us," and presently the cars were rolling down toward the shore road. In five minutes they had stopped before a large bungalow situated far out on one of the rocky points commanding the entire sweep of the bay, and before them riding at anchor was the practice squadron, the good old flagship Olympia, on which Commodore Dewey had fought the battle of Manila Bay, standing bravely out from among her sister ships the Chicago, the Tonopah and the old frigate Hartford anchored along the roadstead.

"Oh, Peggy! Peggy! See them! See them! Don't you love them, every inch of them, from the fighting top to the very anchor chains? I do."

"I ought to," assented Peggy, "for Dad! loves his ship next to me I believe."

"How could he help it?"

They were now hurrying into the cottage where Jerome and Mammy were waiting to welcome them. A couple of servants had been sent over from the Griswold to complete the menage with Mammy and Jerome as commanders-in-chief.

It was a pretty cottage with a broad veranda running around three sides of it and built far out over the water on the front; an ideal spot for a month's outing.

Launches were darting to and from the ships with liberty parties, often with two or three cutters in tow filled with laughing, skylarking midshipmen. On the opposite shore where the old Pequoit House had once stood, was another landing at which many of the ships' boats, or shore boats, were also making landings with parties which had been out to visit the ships. The ships wore a festive air with awnings stretched above their quarter-decks and altogether it was an enchanting picture.

Mammy welcomed her family with enthusiasm, and Jerome with the ceremony he never omitted, and in less time than seemed possible all were settled in their spacious, airy rooms. Mr. and Mrs. Harold had a room looking out over the river, with the two girls next them, while Mrs. Howland, Mr. Stewart, Snap and Constance had rooms just beyond, the three boys being quartered on the floor above.

"Oh, Peggy, isn't it the dearest place you ever saw?" cried Polly, running out on the balcony upon which their room gave. "And there's the dear old flat-iron," the "flat-iron" being the name bestowed by the boys upon the monitor Tonopah because she set so low in the water and was shaped not unlike one, her turrets sticking up like bumpy handles.

"Look, Polly! Look! Some one is wigwagging on the bridge of the Olympia. Oh, Daddy Neil, Daddy Neil, come quickly and tell us what they are saying," she called into the next room.

Neil Stewart hurried out to the balcony, slightly lowering his eyelids as he would have done at sea, a little trick acquired by most men who look across the water.

"Why they are signalling US," he exclaimed. "That's Boynton on the bridge," mentioning an officer whom he knew, "and the chap signalling is - YOU - no, no I don't mean that, I mean it's the chap who ought to be you, that Devon, Deroux, no - Leroux - isn't that his name? The fellow who rigged up in girl's clothes and fooled me to a frazzle. He's saying - what's that? Hold on - Yes! 'Welcome to New London' and - 'Coming on board.' THAT means that a whole bunch will descend upon us tonight I'll bet all I'm worth. Well, let 'em come! Let 'em come! The more the merrier for there's nothing amiss with the commissary department. Here, Happy, Happy, come and answer that signal out yonder. I'm rusty, but you ought to have it down pat."

"Aye, aye, sir," answered Happy, appearing at the window overhead and by some miraculous means scrambling through it and letting himself drop to the balcony where Mr. Stewart and the girls were standing.

"Give me a towel, quick, Peggy."

Peggy rushed for a towel and a moment later the funny wigwag was answering:

"Come along. Delighted."

And that night the bungalow was filled to overflowing, for not only did the boys come, but several officers who had known Mr. Stewart and Mr. Harold for years were eager to renew their acquaintance, and talk over old days.

"And you've come just in time for the regatta. Going to be a big race this year. The men are up at Gales ferry now and look fit to a finish. How are you planning to see it?" asked the captain of the Olympia.

"Haven't planned a thing yet. Why we've only just struck our holding ground, man."

"Good, I'm glad of it. That fixes it all right. You are all to be my guests that day - yes - no protests. Rockhill has gone to Europe and left his launch at my service and she's a jim-dandy, let me tell you. She's a sixty-footer and goes through the water like a knife blade. You'll all come with me and we'll see the show from a private box."

"Can you carry ALL OF US?" asked Peggy incredulously.

"Every last one, little girl, and a dozen more if you like. So fly to the east and fly to the west and then invite the very one whom you love best," answered Captain Boynton, pinching Peggy's velvety cheek.

"Oh, there are so many we love best," she laughed, "that we'd never dare ask them all, would we, Polly?"

"Let's ask all who are here tonight," was Polly's diplomatic answer, "then no one can feel hurt."

"Hoopla!" rose from the other end of the porch where Durand, Ralph, and three of the other boys from the ships were sitting around a big bamboo table drinking lemonade.

And so the party was then and there arranged for New London's big day.

CHAPTER XV

REGATTA DAY

Peggy and Polly scrambled out of bed the morning of the Yale-Harvard crew race, to find all the world sparkling and cool with a stiff breeze from the Sound. It was a wonderful day and already the sight presented in the bay was enough to thrill the dullest soul. During the five days in which "Navy Bungalow," as it had been promptly named by the young people, had been occupied by the congenial party from Annapolis, old friendships had strengthened and new ones ripened, and a happier gathering of people beneath one roof it would have been hard to find. Perfect freedom was accorded every one, and the boys who had just graduated soon found their places with the older officers, for the transition, once the diploma is won, is a swift one. As passed midshipmen and "sure enough" junior officers, they had an established position impossible during their student days in the Academy.

The boys on the practice cruise also felt a greater degree of liberty, and the fact that they were the proteges of Commander Harold and Captain Stewart gave them an entree everywhere.

To Durand the experience was not a new one, for he had the faculty of winning an entree almost anywhere,

Gabrielle E. Jackson

but to Ralph and his roommate, Jean Paul Nicholas, as bright, merry a chap as ever looked frankly into one's face with a pair of the clearest, snappiest blue eyes ever seen, the world was an entirely new one and fairly overflowing with delightful experiences. Then, too, they were now youngsters instead of plebes, and this fact alone would have been almost enough to fill their cups with joy. The other boys who came from the ships had been second-classmen during the past year, but were now in all the glory of first-classmen, and doing their best to make good during the cruise in order to carry off some of the stripes waiting to be bestowed upon the efficient ones during the coming October.

In the two weeks spent with Mrs. Harold at Annapolis, Mrs. Howland had learned to love Peggy Stewart very dearly and Mrs. Harold said:

"Madeline, you have won more from Peggy Stewart than you realize. She has a rarely sweet character, though I am forced to admit that she seems to have been navigating uncharted waters. I have never known a girl of her age to live such an extraordinary life and why she is half as lovable, charming and possessed of so much character, is a problem I have been trying all winter to solve. But I rather dread the next few years for her unless some one both wise and affectionate takes that little clipper ship's helm. She is entirely beyond Harrison and Mammy now, and her father hasn't even a passing acquaintance with his only child. He THINKS he has, and he loves her devotedly, but there's more to Peggy Stewart in one hour than Neil Stewart will discover in years at the rate of two months out of twelve spent with her. I think the world of the child, but Polly is MY girl, and has slipped into Constance's place. I want you to let her stay with me, too. I have been so happy this winter, and she with me, but I wish there was someone to be in Peggy's home, or she could be sent to a good school for a year or two. Sometimes I think that would be the best arrangement in the long run."

Meanwhile Peggy was entirely unaware of the manner in which her future was being discussed and she and Polly were looking forward to regatta day with the liveliest anticipation.

As Peggy and Polly looked out over the bay and up the river that perfect morning Peggy cried:

"Oh, Polly COULD anything be lovelier than this day? The sky is like a blue canopy, not a cloud to be seen, the air just sets one nearly crazy, and that blue, sparkling water makes me long to dive head-first into it."

"Well, why not?" asked Polly. "It is only half past six and loads of time for a dip before breakfast. Let's get into our bathing suits, bang on the ceiling to wake up Happy, Shortie and Wheedles and make them stick their heads out of the window."

It did not take five minutes to carry the suggestion into effect and a golf stick thumping "reveille" under Wheedles' bed effectually brought him back from dreams of Annapolis. Rousing out the other two he stuck a tousled head out of his window to be hailed by two bonny little figures prancing excitedly upon the balcony beneath him.

"Hello, great god Sumnus," cried Polly, "Wake up! Oh, but you do look sleepy. Stir up the others. Peggy and I are going down for a dip before breakfast and to judge by your eyes they need the sand washed out of them."

"Awh! Whow! Oh," yawned Wheedles, striving vainly to keep his mouth closed and to get his eyes opened. Just then two other heads appeared.

"What's doing? House afire?" they asked.

"No, it's the other element - water," laughed Peggy. "Come and get into it. That's what we are going to do. You may think those pink and blue JACKETS you're wearing are the prettiest things in the world - WE know they are part of your graduation "trousseau," but bathing suits are in order just now. So put them on and hurry down."

"Bet your life," was chorused as the three tousled heads vanished.

The average midshipman's "shift" requires as a rule, about two minutes, and passed-middies are no exception. Before it seemed possible three bath-robed figures joined the girls, who had put their raincoats over their bathing suits, and all slipped down to the little beach in front of the cottage and struck out for the float anchored about fifty feet off shore.

What a sight the bay and river presented that morning. Hundreds of beautiful yachts, foregathered from every part of the world, for New London makes a wonderful showing Regatta week, and flying the flags of innumerable yacht clubs, were crowding the roadstead. A more inspiring sight it would be difficult to imagine. Just beyond the float, and lying between the Olympia and Navy Bungalow, the pretty little naptha launch on which Captain Stewart's party were to be Captain Boynton's guests, rode lightly at anchor, her bright work reflecting the sunlight, her awning a-flutter, her signal pennant waving bravely.

"I've GOT to play I'm a porpoise. I've simply GOT to. Come on, Wheedles, nothing else will work off my pent-up excitement," cried Polly, diving off the float to tumble and turn over and over in the water very like the fish she named, for Polly's training with Captain Pennell during the winter had made her almost as much at home in the water as on land and Peggy swam equally well.

While the young people were splashing about Mrs. Harold and Mrs. Howland came out on the piazza to enjoy the sight.

For half an hour the five splashed, dove, and gamboled as carefree as five young seals, and with as much freedom, then all hurried into the bathhouses where Mammy and Jerome had already anticipated their needs by hurrying down with a supply of necessary wearing apparel; a trifling matter quite overlooked by the bathers themselves.

A gayer, heartier, more glowing group of young people than those gathered at the breakfast table could not have been found in New London or anywhere else; certainly not at the Griswold where the majority of them were either satiated society girls whose winters had been spent in a mad social whirl, or the blase city youths who at nineteen had already found life "such a beastly bore."

" Gad, " cried Neil Stewart, slapping Shortie's broad

shoulders, "but it's refreshing to find fellows of your age who can still show up such a glow in their cheeks, and such a light in their eyes, and an enthusiasm so infectious that it sets a-tingle every drop of blood in an old kerfoozalem like me. Hang fast to it like grim death, for you'll never get it back if you once lose it. That old school down there turns out chaps who can get more out of the simple life than any bunch I know of. It may be the simple life in some respects, but it's got a confounded lot of hard work in it all the same, and when you've finished that you're ready to take your fun, and you take it just as hard as you take your work, and I don't want to see a better bunch of men than that system shows. I was over at the hotel last night, talking with four or five chaps, younger than you fellows here, and I swear it made me sick: Bored to extinction doing nothing. I'd like to take 'em on board for just about one month and if they didn't find something doing in a watch or two I'd know why. Keep right on having your fun, you and the girls - yes, GIRLS, not a lot of kids playing at being nerve-racked society women."

"Hear! Hear!" cried Glenn Harold. "What's stirred you up, old man?"

"That bunch over yonder. Keep a little girl as long as you can Peggy, and you, Polly, hold your present course. Who ever charted it for you knew navigation all right."

"I guess mother began it and then turned the job over to Aunt Janet, sir," answered Polly.

"Well, she knew her business all right. I'm mighty sorry she can't be here today to see the race, but when she comes back from Northampton she'll bring that other girl I'm so anxious to know too. By George, the Rowland crowd puts up a good showing, and they seem to know how to choose their messmates too, if I can judge by Hunter."

"Isn't he the dearest brother a girl ever had?" asked Polly enthusiastically, for her love for her brother-in-law was a subject of pleasurable comment to all who knew her.

"One of the best ever, as I hear on all sides," was Captain Stewart's satisfactory answer. "But here comes Boynton. Ahoy! Olympia Ahoy!" he shouted, hurrying out upon the piazza as a launch from the Olympia came boiling "four bells" toward Navy Bungalow's dock, the white clad Jackies looking particularly festive and Captain Boynton of the Olympia with Commander Star of the Chicago sitting aft. They waved their caps gaily and shouted in return.

"Glorious day! Great, isn't it?" as the launch ran alongside the dock and friends hurried down to meet friends.

"We came over to see how early you could be ready. We must get up the course in good season this afternoon in order to secure a vantage point. Mrs. Boynton wants you all - yes - the whole bunch, to come over to the Griswold for an early luncheon. Mrs. Star will be with her and we'll shove off right afterward. Now NO protests," as Captain Stewart seemed inclined to demur.

"All right. Your word goes. "We'll report for duty. What's the hour?"

"Twelve sharp. There's going to be an all-fired jam in that hotel but Mrs. B. has a private dining-room ready for us and has bribed the head waiter to a degree that has nearly proved my ruin. But never mind. We can't see the Yale-Harvard race every day, and a month hence we'll be up in Maine with all this fun behind us."

That luncheon was a jolly one. Captain Boynton had a daughter a little younger than Peggy and Mr. Star a little girl of eight.

Promptly at two the party went down to the Griswold dock, gay with excitement and a holiday crowd embarking in every sort of craft, all bound for the course up the river. The naptha launch had been run alongside the long Griswold pier and it did not take long for Captain Boynton's party to scramble aboard. Captain Boynton, Captain Stewart and the girls went forward, some of the boys making for the bow where the outlook was enough to stir older and far more staid souls than any the Frolic carried that day.

They cast off, and soon were making their fussy way in and out among the hundreds of launches, yachts and craft of every known description.

The crew of the Frolic was a picked one, the coxswain, an experienced hand, as was certainly required THAT day. The pretty launch was dressed in all her bunting, and flying the flag of her club.

Through the mass of festive shipping the launch worked her way, guided by the steady hand of the man at her wheel, his gray eyes alert for every move on port or starboard.

Peggy and Polly were close beside him. Captain Stewart and Captain Boynton stood a little behind watching the girls, whose eager eyes noted every turn of the wheel. An odd light came into Captain Boynton's eyes as he watched them. Presently he asked Peggy:

"Do you think you could handle a launch, little girl?"

"Why - perhaps I could - a little," answered Peggy modestly.

"Why, Peggy Stewart, there isn't a girl in Annapolis who can handle a launch or a sailboat as YOU do," cried Polly, aroused to emphatic protest.

Peggy blushed, and laughingly replied: "Only Polly Howland, the Annapolis Co-Ed."

"Eh? What's that?" asked Captain Boynton.

"Oh, Polly has had a regular course in seamanship, Captain Boynton, and knows just everything."

"Any more than YOU do, miss?" demanded Polly.

"Yes, lots," insisted Peggy.

"Well, I'll wager anything you could take this launch up the river as easily as the coxswain is doing it," was Polly's excited statement.

"How's that, Stewart? Have you been teaching your girl navigation?"

" I hadn't a thing to do with it. It's all due to the good

Gabrielle E. Jackson

friends who have been looking after her while I'VE been shooting up targets. But Polly's right. She CAN handle a craft and so can this little redhead," laughed Captain Stewart, pulling a lock of Polly's hair which the frolicsome wind had loosened.

"By Jove, let's test it. Not many girls can do that trick. Coxswain, turn over the wheel to this young lady, but stand by in case you're needed."

The coxswain looked a little doubtful, but answered: "Aye, aye, sir."

"Oh, ought I?" asked Peggy.

"Get busy, messmate," said Captain Boynton.

The next second the girl was transformed. Tossing her big hat aside and giving her hair a quick brush, she laid firm hold upon the wheel and instantly forgot all else. Her eyes narrowed to a focus which nothing escaped, and Stewart gave a little nod of gratified pride and stepped back a trifle to watch her. Captain Boynton's face showed his appreciation and Polly's was radiant. The old coxswain muttered: "Well, well, you get on to the trick of that, lassie. You might have served on a man-o-war."

They were now well out in the river and making straight for the railway bridge. Peggy alert and absorbed was watching the current as it swirled beneath the arches. "How does the tide set in that middle arch, coxswain?" she asked.

"Keep well to starboard, miss," he answered.

Peggy nodded, and gave an impatient little gesture as a lumbering power boat, outward bound seemed inclined to cut across her course. "What ails that blunderbuss? I have the right of way. Why doesn't he head inshore?" and she signalled sharply on her siren to the landlubber evidently bent upon running down everything in sight, and wrecking the tub he was navigating. Then with a quick motion she flicked over her wheel and rushed by, making as pretty a circle around him as the coxswain himself could have made. "Holy smoke, but ye have given him the go-by in better shape than I could myself. Whoever taught ye?"

"A navy captain down at Annapolis," answered Peggy, as she shot the launch beneath the bridge.

"Well, he did the job all right, all right, and I may as well go back and sit down. Faith, I thought we were as good as stove in when I handed over the wheel to ye, but I'm thinking I can learn a fancy touch or two myself."

"Oh, no, don't go. I don't know the river, you know, though I want to do my best just to make Daddy proud of me," answered Peggy modestly.

"Well then he should be a-yellin' like them crazy loons yonder on the observation train - that's what he should," nodded the coxswain.

Neil Stewart was not yelling, but he wasn't missing a thing, and presently Peggy ran the launch into a clear bit of water near the three-mile flag.

Bringing her around, she issued her orders, her mind too intent upon the business in hand to be conscious that all on the launch had been watching her with absorbing interest. Anchors were thrown over fore and aft in order to hold the launch steady against the current, then turning the wheel over to the admiring coxswain, Peggy wiped her hands upon her handkerchief and holding out her right one to Captain Boynton, said:

"Thank you so much for letting me try. It was perfectly glorious to feel her respond to every touch and thread her way through all that ruck."

"Thank me? Great Scott, child, you've done more for the whole outfit than you guess. Stewart, my congratulations."

Poor Peggy was overcome, but the boys and Polly were alternately running and praising her, every last one of them as proud as possible to call Peggy Stewart chum.

But out yonder the shells were already in the water and the electric spark of excitement had flashed from end to end of that long line of gayly bedecked expectant yachts and launches, as down to them floated the strains of the Yale boating song as it is never sung at any other time, and thousands of eager eyes were peering along the course watching for the first glimpse of the dots which would flash by to victory or defeat.

CHAPTER XVI

THE RACE

The shells had now gotten away and were maneuvering to get into a good position at their stake boats, far beyond the sight of the gay company on hoard the Frolic, which could only guess how things were progressing by the rocketing cheers all along the line of anxiously waiting spectators.

Along the course the launches of the committee were darting thither and yonder like water-bugs in their efforts to keep the course clear. Presently arose the cries:

"They are off! They are off! They are coming! They are coming," and far up the line the puffing of the observation train could be heard with now and again an excited, hysterical tooting of the engine's whistle, as though in the midst of so much excitement it had to give vent to its own.

Presently two dots were visible, looking little more than huge water-bugs in the perspective, the foreshortening changing the long sixty-foot shells into spidery creatures with spreading legs.

The observation train following along the shore

Gabrielle E. Jackson

presented an animated, vari-colored spectacle, with its long chain of cars filled with beautifully gowned women and girls, and men in all the bravery of summer serges and white flannels. Banners were waving and voices cheering, to be caught up and flung back in answering cheers from the craft upon the river.

Peggy and Polly stood as girls so often do in stress of excitement, with arms clasped about each others' waists. The boys stood in characteristic attitudes: Durand with his hands upon his hips - lithe and straight as an arrow, but intent upon the onrushing crews; Shortie with his arm thrown over Wheedles' shoulder subconsciously demonstrating the affection he felt for this chum from whom he would so soon be separated and for how long he could not tell. The friendships formed at the Academy are exceptionally firm ones, but with graduation comes a dividing of the ways sometimes for years, sometimes forever. It is a special provision of Providence that youth rarely dwells upon this fact, and the feeling is invariably expressed by:

"So long! See you later, old man." Captain Stewart and Commander Harold were a striking evidence of this fact. They had not met until years had elapsed and the common tie of daughter and niece had re-united their interests. But, another strange feature; they had as much in common today as though their ways had divided only the week before.

They now stood watching the approaching crews with powerful glasses, their terse comments enlightening their friends as to what was taking place beyond their unaided range of vision. Peggy and Polly were fairly dancing up and down in their eagerness.

On came the shells growing every second more defined in outline, although from their distance from the Frolic their progress seemed slow, only the flashing of the blades in and out of the water indicating that the men were not out for a pleasure pull, and the blue ripples astern telling that sixteen twelve-foot sweeps were pushing that water behind them for all they were worth.

Thus far Harvard was in the lead by half a length, and holding her own as she drew near the three-mile flag, where the Frolic swung and tugged at her anchors. But it must be admitted that the sympathies and hopes of all in the Frolic centered in the Yale shell; a Yale coach had drilled and scolded and "cussed" and petted the Navy boys to victory only a few weeks before, and Ralph, if no one else, felt that all his future rested in the ability of that Yale coach "to knock some rowing sense into his block."

"Daddy Neil! Daddy Neil, yell at them! Yell!" screamed Peggy, breaking away from Polly to run to her father's side and literally shake him, as the crews drew nearer and nearer.

"I AM yelling, honey. Can't you hear me?"

"I mean yell something that will make those Yale men put - put oh, something into their stroke which will overhaul the red blades."

"Ginger? You mean ginger? To make 'em pull like the very - ahem. Like the very dickens? Hi! Shortie, whoop up the Siren - there are only about a dozen of us here but give it hard. Give it for all you're worth when the Yale crew crosses our bow. You girls know it and so do the older women, and the crew can make a try at it. Now be ready. Whoop it up!"

Shortie sprang into position as cheer-leader pro-tem and if wild gyrations and a deep voice lent inspiration certainly nothing more was needed, for as the shells came rushing on

> "Hoo - oo - oo - oo - oooo!
> Hoo - oo - oo - oo - oooo!
> Hoo - oo - oo - oo - oooo!
> Hoo - oo - oo - oo - oooo!
> Navy! Navy! Navy!
> Yale! Yale! Yale!"

was wailed out over the water, and as upon many another occasion back yonder on the old Severn it had acted as a match to gunpowder to a losing cause with the Navy boys, so it now startled the men in the Yale boat, for they had many friends in the Navy School and had heard that yell too often when they were in the lead in some sport not to know the full significance of it. It meant to the losing people: "Get after the other fellows and beat them in spite of all the imps of the lower regions!"

The Yale men had no time to acknowledge the cheer; all their thoughts and energies must center upon the O-n-e, T-w-o, T-h-r-e-e, F-o-u-r, F-i-v-e, etc. of the coxswain and his "Stroke! Stroke! Stroke!" But that yell had done what Peggy hoped and secretly prayed it would:

The long blades flashed in and out of the water quicker and cleaner, cutting down Harvard's lead, until just as they swept by the Frolic that discouraging discrepancy was closed and the two shell's noses were even. Yale had made a gallant spurt.

"Up anchor and after them," ordered Captain Boynton and the crew sprang to obey orders, eagerness to see the finish lending phenomenal speed to their fingers, and the Frolic was soon in hot pursuit of the shells, Yale now pulling a trifle ahead of her adversary in that last fateful mile.

How those eight bare backs swayed back and forth. Harvard's beautiful, long, clean sweep was doing pretty work, but that Siren Yell seemed to have supplied the "ginger" necessary to spur on the Yale men.

"Give 'em another! Give 'em another!" shouted Captain Stewart, as the Frolic came abreast of the Yale crew, and fairly shaking Captain Harold in his excitement.

"Avast there! Give way, man! Do you want to yank me out of my coat?" he laughed.

"I'll yank somebody out of something if those Yale boys don't pull a length ahead of those Johnny Harvards," sputtered Neil Stewart.

"Whoop it up fellows - AND friends. The four N Yell for old Yale," bawled Shortie in order to make himself heard above the din and pandemonium of screaming sirens and the yelling, and in spite of it all the Yale crew heard

> "N - n - n - n!
> A - a - a - a!
> V - v - v - v!

Y - y - y - y!
Yale! Yale! Yale!"

and laid their strength to their sweeps. Chests were heaving and breath coming in panting gasps, but the coxswain of the Yale crew was abreast of number three in the Harvard shell, and inch by inch the space was lengthening in favor of the blue-tipped blades.

"Yale! Yale! Yale!"

yelled the crowd as only such a crowd can yell. Then clear water showed between the shells and the four-mile flag fluttered like a blur as the Yale crew rushed by it. Slower plied the blades, shoulders which had swayed backward and forward in such perfect rhythm drooped, and one or two faces, gray from exhaustion, fell forward upon heaving chests. Then the rowing ceased, the long oars trailed over the water, as Harvard's crew slid by and came to a standstill. Friends flocked to the shells to bring them alongside the floats where, nerve-force coming to the rescue of physical exhaustion, the big fellows managed to scramble to the floats and fairly hug each other as they did an elephantine dance in feet from which some stockings were sagging, and some gone altogether. But who cared whether legs were bare or covered!

The Frolic came boiling up to the float at a rate calculated to smash things to smithereens if she did not slow down at short order, everybody yelling, everybody shouting like bedlamites.

"Best ever! Best ever! The Siren started it and the Four N. did the trick!" shouted Captain Stewart, while all the others cheered and congratulated in chorus.

"Give 'em again. Give 'em again. By Jove, I'm going to get up a race of my own and all you fellows will have to come to yell for us," cried Captain Boynton, and again the Navy Yell sent a thrill through those weary bodies upon the float. Then gathering together all the "sand" left in them they gave the old Eli Yell for their friends of the Navy with more spirit than seemed possible after such a terrific ordeal as they had just undergone.

And all those months of training, all that endless grind of hard work, for a test which had lasted but a few minutes, ending in a certain victory for one shell and a certain defeat for the other, since victory surely could not possibly result for both.

"See you all at the Griswold tonight," called Captain Boynton, as the launch shoved off and got under way.

"Sure thing! Have our second wind by that time we hope," were the cheery answers.

"Take the helm again, little skipper," ordered Captain Boynton. "Your Daddy is just dying to have you but modesty forbids him to even look a hint of it."

"May I really?" asked Peggy.

"Get busy," and Peggy laughed delightedly as she took the wheel from the coxswain who handed it over with:

"Now I'll take a lesson from a man-o-war's lassie."

Shortie, Happy and Wheedles had now gone aft to "be luxurious" they said, for wicker chairs there invited relaxation and the ladies were more than comfortable.

Ralph, Durand and Jean had gone forward to the wheel to watch the little pilot's work, Durand's expressive face full of admiration for this young girl who had grown to be his good comrade.

Durand was not a "fusser," but he admired Peggy Stewart more than any girl he had ever known, and the friendship held no element of silly sentimentality.

How bonny they both looked, and how strikingly alike. Could there, after all, have been any kindred drop of blood in their ancestry? It did not seem possible, yet how COULD two people look so alike and not have some kinship to account for it?

Peggy was not conscious of Durand's close scrutiny. She was too intent upon taking the Frolic back to the Griswold's dock without being stove in, for in the homeward rush of the sightseers, there seemed a very good chance of such a disaster.

Nevertheless, there always seems to be a special Providence watching over fools, and to judge by the manner in which some of those launches were being handled, that same Providence had all it could handle that afternoon.

They had gone about half the distance, and Peggy was having all she wanted to do to keep clear of one particularly erratic navigator, her face betokening her contempt for the wooden-headed youth at the helm.

The badly handled launch was about thirty feet long, and carrying a heavier load than was entirely safe. She was yawing about erratically, now this way, now that.

"Well, that gink at the helm is a mess and no mistake," was Durand's scornful comment. "What the mischief is he trying to do with that tub anyhow?"

"Wreck it, ruin a better one, and drown his passengers, I reckon," answered Peggy.

"And look at that little child. Haven't they any better sense than to let her clamber up on that rail?" exclaimed Polly, for just as the launch in question was executing some of its wildest stunts, a little girl, probably six years of age, had scrambled up astern and was trying to reach over and dabble her hands in the water.

"They must be seven kinds of fools," cried Durand. "Say, Peggy, there's going to be trouble there if they don't watch out."

But Peggy had already grown wise to the folly - yes, rank heedlessness - on board the other launch. If any one had the guardianship of that child she was certainly not alive to the duty.

"I'm going to slow down a trifle and drop a little astern," she said quietly to Durand. "Don't say a word to any one else but stand by in case that baby falls overboard; they are not taking any more notice of her than if she didn't belong to them. I never knew anything so outrageous. What sort of people can they be, any way?"

"Fool people," was Durand's terse rejoinder and his remark seemed well merited, for the three ladies on board were chatteringly oblivious of the child's peril, and the men were not displaying any greater degree of sense.

Peggy kept her launch about a hundred feet astern. They had passed the bridge and were nearing the broader reaches of the river where ferry boats were crossing to and fro, and the larger excursion boats which had brought throngs of sightseers to New London were making the navigation of the stream a problem for even more experienced hands, much less the callow youth who was putting up a bluff at steering the "wash tub," as Ralph called it.

The older people in the Frolic were not aware of what was happening up ahead. The race was ended, they had been tinder a pretty high stress of excitement for some time, and were glad to settle down comfortably and leave the homeward trip to Peggy and the coxswain who was close at hand. Never a thought of disaster entered their minds.

Then it came like a flash of lightning:

There was a child's pathetic cry of terror; a woman's wild, hysterical shriek and shouts of horror from the near-by craft.

In an instant Durand was out of his white service jacket, his shoes were kicked off and before a wholesome pulse could beat ten he was overside, shouting to Peggy as he took the plunge:

"Follow close!"

"I'm after you," was the ringing answer.

"Heaven save us!" cried Captain Stewart, springing to

his feet, while the others started from their chairs.

"Trust him. He is all right, Daddy. I've seen him do this sort of thing before," called Peggy, keeping her head and handling her launch in a manner to bring cheers from the other boats also rushing to the rescue.

It was only the work of a moment for Durand swimming as he could swim, and the next second he had grasped the child and was making for the Frolic, clear-headed enough to doubt the chance of aid being rendered by the people on the launch from which the child had fallen, but absolutely sure of Peggy's cooperation, for he had tested it under similar conditions once before when a couple of inexperienced plebes had been capsized from a canoe on the Severn, and Peggy, who had been out in her sailboat at the time, had sped to their rescue. A boat-hook was promptly held out to the swimmer and he and his burden were both safe on board the Frolic a moment later, neither much the worse for their dip, though the child was screaming with terror, answering screams from one of the women in the other launch indicating that she had some claim to the unfortunate one.

"She's all right. Not a hair harmed. Keep cool and we'll come alongside," ordered Captain Stewart. "Not the least harm done in the world."

But the woman continued to shriek and rave until Mrs. Harold said:

"I would like to shake her soundly. If she had been paying any attention to the child the accident never could have happened."

The dripping baby was transferred to her mother, Captain Harold had clapped Durand on the back and cried: "Boy, you're a trump of the first water," and the rest of the party were telling Peggy that she was "a brick" and "a first-class sport," and "a darling," according to the vocabulary or sex of the individual, when the second feminine occupant of the launch which had been the cause of all the excitement, electrified every one on the Frolic by exclaiming:

"Why, Neil! Neil Stewart! Is it possible after all these years? Don't you know me? Don't you know Katherine? Peyton's wife!"

For a moment Neil Stewart looked nonplussed. His only brother had married years before. Neil had attended the wedding, meeting the bride then, and only twice afterward, for his brother had died two years after his marriage and Neil had never since laid eyes upon Peyton's wife. If the truth must be told he had not been eager to, for she was not the type of woman who attracted him in the least. Yet here she was before him. By this time the launches had been run up to one of the docks upon the West shore of the Thames. Naturally, both consolation for the emotional mother of the child as well as introductions were now in order, Mrs. Harold and Captain Stewart offering their services. These, however, were declined, but Mrs. Peyton Stewart embraced the opportunity to rhapsodize over "that darling child who had handled the launch with such marvelous skill and been instrumental in saving sweet little Clare's life." Durand, drying off in the launch, seemed to be quite out of her consideration in the scheme of things, for which Durand was duly thankful, for he had taken one of his swift, inexplicable aversions to her. But Madam continued to gash over poor Peggy until that modest little girl was well-nigh beside herself.

"And to think you are right here and I have not been aware of it. Oh, I must know that darling child of whose existence I have actually been ignorant. I shall never, never cease to reproach myself."

Neil Stewart did not inquire upon what score, but as soon as it could be done with any semblance of grace, bade his undesirable relative farewell, promising to "give himself the pleasure of calling the following day."

"And be sure *I* shall not lose sight of THAT darling girl again," Mrs. Peyton Stewart assured him.

"I'm betting my hat she won't either," was Durand's comment to Wheedles, "and I'd also bet there's trouble in store for Peggy Stewart if THAT femme once gets her clutches on her. Ugh! She's a piece of work.

"A rotten, bad piece, I'd call it," answered Wheedles under his breath.

When Mr. and Mrs. Harold, Captain Stewart and Peggy returned to the launch one might have thought that they, instead of Durand, had been plunged overboard. They seemed dazed, and the run across to the Griswold dock was less joyous than the earlier portion of the day had been.

CHAPTER XVII

SHADOWS CAST BEFORE

Captain Boynton as host entertained the launch party at dinner at the Griswold that evening, and later all attended the dance given in honor of the winning crew.

Many of the Yale and Harvard men were old friends of the midshipmen, having been to Annapolis a number of times either to witness or participate in some form of athletics. So old friendships were renewed, and new ones made, though, in some way Peggy and Polly felt less at home with the college men than with "our boys," as they both called all from Annapolis, notwithstanding the fact that "our boys" were in some instances the seniors of the college men. But the Academy life is peculiar in that respect, and tends to extremes. Where the collegian from the very beginning of his career is permitted to go and come almost at will, and as a result of that freedom of action attains a liberty which, alack, has been known to degenerate into license, the midshipman must conform to the strictest discipline, his outgoings limited, with the exception of one month out of the twelve, to the environs of a little, undeveloped town, and with every single hour of the twenty-four accounted for. Yet, on the other hand he must at once shoulder responsibilities which would make the average collegian think twice before he bound himself to assume them.

And the result is an exceptional development: they are boys at heart, but men in their ability to face an issue. Ready to frolic, have "a rough house," and set things humming at the slightest provocation, but equal to meet a crisis when one must be met and - with very rare exceptions - gentlemen in word and deed.

Peggy's and Polly's chums during the winter just past had been chosen from the best in the Academy, and it was no wonder they drew very sharp, very critical comparisons when brought in touch with other lads. In Peggy's case it was all a novelty, though Polly had known boys all her life.

Nevertheless, the ball given at the Griswold would have been joy unalloyed but for one fly in the pot of ointment: A most insistent, buzzing fly, too, in the form of Mrs. Peyton Stewart.

Perhaps while all the world is a-tiptoe in the packed ballroom, or crowding the broad piazzas of the hotel, this will be an opportune moment in which to drop a word regarding Mrs. Peyton Stewart.

As lads, Neil Stewart and his brother had been devotedly attached to each other. Peyton was five years Neil's junior, and Neil fairly adored the bright little lad. Naturally, Neil had entered the Naval Academy while Peyton was still a small boy at boarding-school. Then Peyton went to college and at the ripe age of twenty-two, married.

Had the marriage been a wise one, or one likely to help make a man of the heedless, harum-scarum Peyton, his family, and his brother, would probably have accepted the situation with as good a grace as possible. But it was NOT wise: it was the very essence of folly, for the girl was nearer Neil's age than Peyton's, and came of a family which could never have had anything in common with Peyton Stewart's. She was also entirely frivolous, if not actually designing. Neil was the only member of his family who attended the wedding, which took place in a small New Jersey town, and, as has been stated, had seen his undesirable sister-in-law only twice after her wedding-day. Upon one occasion by accident, and upon the last at his brother's death, only two years after the marriage, and had then and there resolved never to see her again if he could possibly help it, for never had one person rubbed another the wrong way as had Mrs. Peyton rubbed her brother-in-law.

Naturally, Peyton had received his share of his inheritance upon the death of his parents, but Neil had inherited Severndale, so while Madam Peyton Stewart was not by any means lacking in worldly goods, she had nothing like the income her brother-in-law enjoyed. But she was by no means short-sighted, and like a flash several thoughts had entered her head when chance brought her in touch with him. She had never been of the type which lets a good opportunity slip for lack of prompt action, so in spite of her hostess' rather excited frame of mind as the result of the afternoon's accident, she persuaded her to attend the ball at the Griswold that evening.

She must have something to divert her thoughts from the horror of that precious child's disaster and miraculous rescue from death, she urged, that same child, as a matter of fact, being as gay and chipper as though a header from the stern of a crowded launch into a more crowded river was a mere daily incident in her life.

So there sat Madam, gorgeous in white satin and silver, plying her fan and her tongue with equal energy.

Presently Peggy danced by with Durand, not a few eyes following the beautiful young girl and handsome boy, and to an individual those who saw them decided that they were brother and sister. This was Mrs. Stewart's opportunity and she made the most of it: Turning to a lady beside her she gurgled:

"Oh, that darling child. She is my only niece though I have never met her until this very afternoon. Isn't she a beauty? THINK what a sensation she will be sure to create a year or two hence when she comes out. Don't you envy me? for, of course, there is no one else to introduce her to society. Her mother died years ago."

"And the young man with her?" questioned the lady, wondering why the darling niece had not figured more prominently in the aunt's life hitherto. "Is he her brother?"

"No. He is the hero of the day. The young naval cadet [save the mark!] who so nobly sprang overboard after sweet little Clare and saved her under such harrowing circumstances. Isn't he simply stunning! Have you ever seen a more magnificent figure? I think he is the handsomest thing I've ever laid my eyes upon. And so devoted to dear Peggy. And they say he has a fortune in his own right. But, that is a minor consideration; the dear child is an heiress herself. Magnificent old home in Maryland and, and, oh, all that, don't you know."

Madam's information concerning her niece's affairs seemed to have grown amazingly since that chance encounter during the afternoon.

At that moment the dance came to an end and by evil chance Peggy and Durand were not ten feet from Mrs. Stewart. She beckoned to them and, of course, there was nothing to do but respond. They at once walked over to her.

"Oh, Mrs. Latimer, let me present my dear niece Miss Stewart to you, and Peggy darling, I MUST know this young hero. You dear, dear boy, weren't you simply petrified when you saw that darling child plunge overboard? You are a wonder. A perfect wonder of heroism. Of course the girls are just raving over you. How could they help it? Uniforms, brass buttons, the gallant rescuer and - now turn your head the other way because you are not supposed to hear this - all the gifts and graces of the gods. Ah, Peggy, I suspect you have rare discrimination even at YOUR age, and well - Mr. Leroux - YOU have not made any mistake, I can assure you."

Perhaps two individuals who have suddenly stepped into a hornet's nest may have some conception of Peggy's and Durand's sensations. Peggy looked absolutely, hopelessly blank at this volley. Durand's face was first a thunder-cloud and then became crimson, but not on his own account: Durand was no fool to the ways of foolish women; his mortification was for Peggy's sake; he loathed the very thought of having her brought in touch with such shallowness, exposed to such vulgarity, and the charm of their rarely frank intercourse invaded by suggestions of silly sentimentality. Thus far there had never been a hint, nor the faintest suggestion of it; only the most loyal good fellowship; and his own attitude toward Peggy Stewart was one of the highest esteem for a fine, well-bred girl and the tenderest sense of protection for her lonely, almost orphaned position. He looked at Mrs. Peyton Stewart with eyes which fairly blazed contempt and she had the grace to color tinder his gaze, boy of barely nineteen that he was.

"And you are going to let me know you better, aren't you, dear?" persisted Mrs. Stewart. "I am coming to see you. Do ask father to come and talk with me. There are a thousand questions I must ask him, and innumerable incidents of old times to discuss."

"Captain Stewart is just across the room. I will tell him you are anxious to see him, Mrs. Stewart, and then I must take you to Mrs. Harold, Peggy, or the other fellows will never find you in this jam," and away fled Durand, quick to find a loophole of escape. Whether Neil Stewart appreciated his zeal in serving the family cause is open to speculations, but it served the turn for the moment. Neil Stewart was obliged to cross the room and talk to his sister-in-law, said sister-in-law taking the initiative to rise at his approach, place her hand upon his arm, and say:

"Dear Neil, what a delight after all these years. But pray take me outside. It is insufferably oppressive in here and I have so much I wish to say to you."

Just what "dear Neil's" innermost thoughts were need not be conjectured. He escorted the lady from the big ballroom, and Durand whisked Peggy away to Mrs. Harold, though he said nothing to the girl - he was raging too fiercely inwardly, and felt sure if he said anything he would say too much. Nor was Peggy her usual self. She seemed obsessed by a forewarning of evil days ahead. Durand handed her over to the partner who was waiting for her, and saw her glide away with him, then slipping into a vacant chair behind Mrs. Harold, who for the moment happened to be alone, he said:

"Little Mother, have you ever been so rip-snorting mad that you have wanted to smash somebody and cut loose for fair, and felt as if you'd burst if you couldn't?"

The words were spoken in a half-laughing tone, but Mrs. Harold turned to look straight into the dark eyes so near her own.

"What has happened, son?" she asked in the quiet voice which always soothed his perturbed spirit. He repeated the conversation just heard, punctuating it with a few terse comments which revealed volumes to Mrs. Harold. Her face was troubled as she said:

"I don't like it. I don't like it even a little bit. I'm afraid trouble is ahead for that little girl. Oh, if her father could only be with her all the time. Outsiders can do so little because their authority is so limited and those who HAVE the authority are either too guileless or debarred by their stations. Dr. Llewellyn, Harrison and Mammy are the only ones who have the least right to say one word, and - "

Mrs. Harold ceased and shrugged her shoulders in a manner which might have been copied from Durand himself.

"Yes, I know who you mean. And Peggy is one out of

a thousand. She and Polly too. Great Scott, there isn't an ounce of nonsense in their heads, and if that old fool - I beg your pardon," cried Durand, fussed at his break, but Mrs. Harold nodded and said:

"There are times when it is excusable to call a spade a spade."

"Well," continued Durand, "if that femme starts in to talk such rot to Peggy it's going to spoil everything. Why, you never heard such confounded foolishness in all your life."

"Come and walk on the terrace with me, laddie, and cool off both mentally and physically. I know just how you feel and I wish I could see the way to ward off the inevitable - at least that which intuition hints to be inevitable -

"And that is?" asked Durand anxiously.

"Child, you have been like a son to me for two years. Peggy has grown almost as dear to me as Polly. I long to see that rare little girl blossom into a fine woman and she will if wisely guided, but with such a person as her aunt - "

"You don't for a moment think she will go and camp down at Severndale?" demanded Durand, stopping stock-still in consternation at the picture the words conjured up.

"I don't KNOW a thing! Not one single thing, but I am gifted with an intuition which is positively painful at times," and Mrs. Harold resumed her walk with a petulant little stamp.

Nor was her intuition at fault in the present instance. In some respects Neil Stewart was as guileless and unsuspicious as a child, but Madam Stewart was far from guileless. She was clever and designing to a degree, and before that conversation upon the Griswold piazza, ended she had so cleverly maneuvered that she had been invited to spend the month of September at Severndale, and that was all she wanted: once her entering wedge was placed she was sure of her plans. At least she always HAD been, and she saw no reason to anticipate failure now.

But she did not know Peggy Stewart. She thought she had read at a glance the straightforward, modest little girl, but the real Peggy was not to be understood in the brief period of four hours.

Meanwhile, Peggy was blissfully unaware of her impending fate, and had almost dismissed Mrs. Stewart's very existence from her thoughts. She and Polly were dancing away the hours in all the joy of fifteen summers, and rumors of a wonderful plan were afloat for the following day. This was no more nor less than a cutter race between the midshipmen of the Olympia and the Chicago. For days the two crews had been practising and were only waiting for the big day to come and pass before holding their own contest.

The Chicago really had the picked men, most of them being the regular crew men, and while pulling in a cutter is a far cry from pulling in a shell, nevertheless, the work of trained men usually counts in the long run, and the boys and the Jackies had bet everything they owned, from their best shoes to a month's pay, upon the victory of the Chicago's crew.

But the Olympia boys "were lyin' low, an' playin' sly." They had but one crew man in their cutter, but he was "a jim dandy," being no less than Lowell, the stroke oar of the Navy crew, and a man who could "put more ginger into a boatload of fellows than any other in the outfit," so his chums averred.

Durand was on the Olympia's crew, and Durand's shoulders were worth considerable to any crew.

Nicholas was on the "Old Chi," Ralph on the Olympia, so the forces were about equally divided, and the girls were nearly distracted over the issue, for if they could have had the decision both would have been victorious.

The following morning dawned as sparkling and clear as the previous one. "Regular Harold weather," the boys pronounced it, owing to the fact that rarely had Mrs. Harold planned a frolic of any sort back yonder in Annapolis without the weather clerk smiling upon it.

When "Colors" came singing across the water at eight o'clock, up went the squadron's bunting in honor of the day, and a pretty picture the ships presented dressed from stem to stern in their gay, varicolored flags.

The race would take place at three o'clock in the afternoon but a preliminary pull over the course was in order for the morning, and Captain Boynton of the Olympia and Captain Star of the Chicago were as eager to have all conditions favorable, and the lads "fit to a finish," as though their ages, like those of the contestants were within the first score of life's journey. So their launches were ordered out to watch that morning practice and they ran and jeered each other like a couple of schoolboys out for a lark, and that attitude did more to put spirit in the boys, to establish good feeling and the determination to "Put up a showing for the Old Chi" or "that fighting machine of the old man's," the "old man" being their term of affection for Admiral Dewey, than all the "cussing out" in the English vocabulary could have done.

CHAPTER XVIII

YOU'VE SPOILED THEIR TEA PARTY

So absolutely confident of winning were the people, officers, midshipmen and crew on board the Chicago that they had made all their plans for the elaborate tea and dance to be given on board the ship of the winning crew.

Boatloads of Jackies had been sent ashore for evergreens, and a force of men had been put to work decorating the quarter-deck, the wardroom and the steerage until the ship presented a wonderful picture. The dance was to be held on the quarter-deck of the ship of the victorious crew immediately after the race, so the preparations were elaborate and hopes more than sanguine. Already the Chicago's officers mentally pictured the gay gathering upon her tastefully decorated decks; saw the handsomely gowned chaperones and the daintily clad girls in all the bravery of summer gowns dancing to the strains of the ship's band. Oh, it was the prettiest mental vision imaginable!

And on the old Olympia? That stately veteran of Manila Bay upon whose bridge his loyal, devoted admirers had outlined in brass-headed nails the very spot where Commodore Dewey's feet had rested as he spoke the memorable words:

"When you are ready you may fire, Gridley."

And the Olympia's personnel? The admiral of the fleet, the captain and the officers straight down to the very stokers? Well, THEY had an idea of what the Olympia's men were worth when it came to the scratch and a few things were privately moving forward which might have made the Chicago's personnel sit up and take notice had they found time to do so.

There were no EVERGREENS brought over the side, it is true, but launches had been darting to and fro with systematic regularity, and each time they came from New London significant-looking boxes, important junior officers, and odd freight came, too, but no one was the wiser. Not only were awnings spread fore and aft, but they were hung in such a way that passing craft, however curious the occupants, could not see what might be taking place on board.

But with five bells came a revelation. A steady line of launches put off to the shore, some to the east, some to the west, to return with a gay freight, and as they came up the starboard gangway the festive femininity broke into rapturous exclamations, for on every side were roses! Red roses, white roses, pink roses, pale yellow roses, begged, bought or - hush! - from every farm-house within a radius of five miles, and every nook and corner of the deck was made snug and attractive with bunting, or rug-covered - well, if not chairs, improvised seats which served the purpose equally well and from which "the get-away" could be clearly seen, the course being a triangular one, starting on the port side of the Olympia and ending on the starboard bow. The Chicago, with all her bravery, lacked the position held by the Olympia.

Captain Stewart's party were the guests of the Olympia and had come aboard early.

Peggy and Polly were wild with excitement. At least Polly was; Peggy took her pleasures with less demonstration.

The cutter crews were already in their boats and ready to pull out to the starter's launch which bobbed gaily within easy range of the quarter-deck.

Peggy and Polly hung over the rail calling cheery farewells to Durand and Lowell and telling the others that they would never forgive them if they did not win the trophy.

"Win! Win! Fill up that tin cup right now and have it ready to hand over when we come back the proud victors of the day, for we'll be thirsty and you can just bet we're going to come back in that fascinating guise - winners, we mean. What? Let those lobsters from the 'Chi' beat us out? Not on your life! You just watch us play with them, and pull all around them," shouted Lowell as the cutter shoved off at the coxswain's word.

Meanwhile the Chicago's cutter had taken. her berth and was ready for the send-off from the committee's launch.

Now a cutter race is no holiday pastime but a long pull and a strong pull from start to finish, for a cutter weighs something over and above a racing shell, to say nothing of her lines being designed for service in stress rather than for a holiday fete. Add to the weight of the boat herself her freight of twelve men, and all pretty husky fellows, and you've got some pulling ahead in order to push that boat through a given distance of water.

If all the civil world had been on the alert during the previous day's contest, certainly all the little Navy world assembled at New London was on the alert that afternoon. The decks of the Chicago and Olympia were crowded with friends. The ships' launches were darting about like distracted water-bugs, and innumerable "shore boats" were bringing guests from every direction.

Presently, however, the course was cleared, the signals given and the heavy oars took the water as only "man-o-war's men's" oars ever take it: as though one brain controlled the actions of the entire crew.

The start was pretty even, the huge sweeps dipping into the water simultaneously and cleanly. Then the Chicago's men began to pull slowly away from the Olympia's, the coxswain right at the outset hitting up the stroke faster than the Olympia's coxswain considered good judgment so early in the race, for that triangle had three sides, as is the rule of triangles, and each side presented a pretty good distance.

But the people on the Chicago were cheering and yelling like bedlamites, pleased to the very limit to see their men putting up such a showing, and confident of their ability to hold it to the finish. They did not pause to reason that they had begun at a stroke which meant just a degree more endurance than most men are equal to, but they were sanguine that their ship was to hold a function in their honor.

Just astern the Chicago's boat the Olympia's coxswain

was keeping up his steady "Stroke! Stroke! Stroke! Stroke!" which sent the boat boiling through the water as though propelled by a gasoline engine. The Olympia's men were holding their own if not breaking a record.

"Hold her steady. Keep the stroke. We won't try to set the Thames afire - not YET," were the coach's significant words from his launch.

Lowell nodded quick understanding but kept his steady weight against the oar which was setting the stroke for the men behind him, and Durand's eyes hardly left the sway and swing of that splendid broad back just in front of him as on they rushed to the first flag-boat, making the turn of the triangle just a length astern of the Chicago's men, and amidst the cries of:

"Hit it up, Olympia! Overhaul 'em! Pull down that lead!" from the launch following, in which several officers were yelling like Comanches.

"Takes better men. You didn't know how to pick 'em," were the taunting cries from the Chicago's launch on their starboard beam.

"Wait till they round the next stake-boat. They're only playing with you now."

"Playing OUT? They've got to do better than this to overhaul US. We are rowing some," were the laughing answers.

"Now we'll play for fair. Hit her up to thirty-six," was the order of the Olympia's coxswain, and the oars flashed response to the order, the cutter seeming to fly.

There was a quick exclamation from the coxswain of the Chicago's cutter, a sharp command, and the stroke jumped to thirty-eight which sent the boat boiling forward. Another command on the Olympia's as the second stake boat was neared and the Olympia's crew was holding it at forty, a slip to tell, and the boats rounded the second stake-boat bows even.

Then came the home stretch; the last telling, racking effort of the two-mile triangle. The Chicago was still pulling a splendid thirty-eight as they swept by the stake-boat, but once the turn was made oars flashed up to forty-two, for the Olympia's nose had forged half a length ahead after that turn.

Meantime pandemonium had cut loose in the launches as well as on board the ships, and if yelling, hooting, or calls through megaphones could put power into a stroke, certainly no inspiration was wanting.

Half the last stretch was covered, the lads rowing in splendid form when the Chicago's men started in to break the record and their launch went mad as they spurted to forty-six to overhaul their rival's lead. But a forty-six stroke is just a trifle more than can be held in a heavy cutter with twelve, fourteen and sixteen-foot oars weighing many pounds each; it simply could not be held.

"Give 'em forty-two for a finish, fellows," bawled the Olympia's coxswain through his megaphone, literally pro bono publico. And forty-two did the trick, for forty-six could not be held, and the Olympia's cutter swept past the stake-boat a length in the lead, while Captain Boynton on the bridge beside the admiral of the fleet fairly jumped up and down.

Alas, and alack for the dance on board the Chicago and the tea to be served to her admiring guests!

One of the conditions of that tea and dance was victory with a capital V for the hosts.

"Bring 'em aboard! Bring 'em aboard! Pass the order," rumbled the admiral.

"Just as they are!" questioned Boynton, not quite sure that he understood aright.

"Yes! Yes! Bring 'em aboard!"

"What will the ladies say?" gasped Boynton. "These rowing togs are rather sketchy."

"Hang their clothes! Get 'em some. Pass the word, man. Bring them up the STARBOARD GANGWAY. Bring 'em up, I say, and get down there to welcome them! They own the ship and everything on board!"

Boynton lost no time in passing the word and hurrying down to greet the winning crew and it seemed as though the whole personnel of the old Olympia had gone stark mad.

But to see and hear was to obey and the Olympia's lads, clad in raiment conspicuous principally for its limitations, came piling up the sacred starboard gangway to be met by Captain Boynton who grasped each hand in turn as he shouted:

"You're a bunch worth while! You spoiled their tea party! You busted up their dance, confound you, you scamps! You did 'em up in shape and WE'RE the whole show! Now go below and get fit to be seen, then come back and let the ladies feed you and make fools of you, for they'll DO it all right."

And they were fed! They were ready to be. A pull over such a course means an appetite, but whether these level-headed chaps were made fools of is open to question.

It was long after dark before that frolic ended, and the ships were a fairy spectacle of electric lights, the band's strains floating across the water as light feet tripped to the inspiring strains of waltz or two-step.

That was one of the happiest afternoons and evenings Peggy and Polly had ever known, and so passed many another, for Neil Stewart meant that month to be a memorable one for Peggy, little guessing how soon a less happy one would dawn for her, or how unwittingly he had laid the train for it.

For two weeks there were lawn fetes at Navy Bungalow, long auto trips through the beautiful surrounding country and the delightfully cosy family gatherings which all so loved.

After Gail's graduation Mrs. Howland returned bringing that golden-haired lassie with her, Snap and Constance coming too.

Gail's introduction to the circle was a funny one:

Captain Stewart had been curious to see whether "Howland number four would uphold the showing of the family," as he teasingly told Polly, and Polly who was immensely proud of her pretty sister had brindled and protested that: "Gail was the very best looking one of the family."

"Then she must be going some," he insisted.

She was a sunny, bonny sight in spite of a dusty ride down from Northampton, and Captain Stewart was at the steps to help her from the auto which had been sent up to the New London station to meet her. She stepped out after her mother and Constance, but before Mrs. Howland had a chance to present her Captain Stewart laid a pair of kindly hands upon her shoulders, held her from him a moment, peering at her from under his thick eyebrows in a manner which made a pretty color mantle her cheeks, then said with seeming irrelevance:

"No, the Howland family doesn't lie, but on the other hand they don't invariably convey the whole truth. You'll pass, little girl. Yes, you'll pass, and you don't look a day older than Polly and Peggy even if you are hiding away a sheepskin somewhere in that suitcase yonder. Yes, I'll adopt you as my girl, and by crackey I'm going to seal it," and with that he took the bonny face in both hands and kissed each rosy cheek.

Poor Gail, if the skies had dropped she couldn't have been more nonplussed. She had heard a good deal of the people she was to visit but had never pictured THIS reception, and for once the girl who had been president of her class and carried off a dozen other honors, was as fussed as a schoolgirl.

Peggy came to her rescue.

Running up to her she slipped her arms about her and cried:

"Don't mind Daddy Neil. We are all wild to know you and we're just BOUND to love you. How could we help it? You belong to us now, you know. Come with me. You are to have the room right next ours - Polly's and mine, I mean - and everything will be perfectly lovely."

Within three days after Gail's arrival Happy, Wheedles and Shortie had to leave for their own homes, as their families were clamoring for some of their society during that brief month's leave before they joined their ships. But fortune favored them in one respect, for Happy and Wheedles were ordered to the Connecticut, the flag-ship of the Atlantic fleet, and Shortie to Snap's ship, the Rhode Island in the same fleet. So, contrary to the usual order of things where men in the Academy have been such chums, their ways would not wholly divide.

Two weeks later the practice ships weighed anchor for Newport, and the party at Navy Bungalow was broken up. Mrs. Howland, Constance, Gail and Snap returned to Montgentian. Captain Stewart and Captain Harold were obliged to rejoin their ships, Mrs. Harold, with Polly and Peggy, going on to Newport, thence along the coast, following the practice squadron until its return to Annapolis the last day of August when all midshipmen go on a month's leave and the Academy is deserted.

Mrs. Harold was to spend September with her sister, a pleasure upon which she had long counted. Peggy was invited to join her, but alas! Captain Stewart had rendered THAT impossible by asking his sister-in-law to pass September at Severndale.

Of this Peggy had not learned at once, but was bitterly disappointed when she did, though she strove to conceal it from her father, when, too late, he awakened to what he had done.

Mrs. Stewart had contrived to spend as many hours as possible at Navy Bungalow, but she had certainly not succeeded in winning the friendship of its inmates, and Neil Stewart bitterly regretted the impulse which had prompted him to invite her to Severndale. When too late he realized that he had fallen into a cleverly planned trap, dragging Peggy with him. And what was still worse, that there would be no one at hand to help her out of the situation into which his short-sightedness had involved her. As a last resort he wrote to Dr. Llewellyn:

"I've been seven kinds of a fool. Watch out for Peggy. She's up against it, I am afraid, and it is all my doing. I'll write you at length later. Meanwhile, I'm afraid there'll be ructions."

Poor Dr. Llewellyn was hopelessly bewildered by that letter and prepared for almost anything.

Mrs. Harold and Polly bade Peggy good-bye at New York. Jerome and Mammy acting as her body-guard upon the homeward journey.

It was a hard wrench, and the two girls who had been such close companions for so long felt the separation keenly.

"But you know we'll meet in October and have all next winter before us," were Polly's optimistic parting words, little guessing how the coming winter would be changed for both her and Peggy.

It had been arranged that Mrs. Stewart should arrive at Severndale on the fifth of September. Peggy reached there on the second and in a half-hearted way went about her preparations for receiving her aunt.

Nor were Mammy and Jerome more enthusiastic. They had pretty thoroughly sized up their expected guest while at New London.

Nevertheless, noblesse oblige was the watchword at Severndale.

CHAPTER XIX

BACK AT SEVERNDALE

The first two days of Peggy's return to Severndale were almost overwhelming for the girl. True, Dr. Llewellyn met and welcomed her, and strove in his gentle, kindly manner to make the lonely home-coming a little less lonely. It was all so different from what she had anticipated. That he was there to welcome her at all was a mere chance. He had planned a trip north and completed all his arrangements, when an old, and lifelong friend fell desperately ill. Deferring his trip for the friend's sake, Neil Stewart's letter caught him before his departure, and after reading that his own pleasures and wishes were set aside. Duty, which had ever been his watchword, held him at Severndale.

"When questioned by him - circumspectly it is true - Peggy's answers conveyed no idea of pending trouble, nor did they alter his charitable view of the world or his fellow beings.

"Why, Filiola, I think it must be the very happiest solution of the situation here: I am getting too old and prosy to make life interesting for you; your father will not be retired for several years yet, so there is little hope of your claiming his companionship; Mrs. Harold is a most devoted friend, but friendships in the service must so often be broken by the exigencies of the duties; she may be compelled to leave Annapolis at almost any time, and if she is, your friend Polly will be obliged to leave also. Why, little one, it seems to me quite providential that you should have met your aunt in New London and that she will visit you here," and good Dr. Llewellyn stroked with gentle touch the pretty brown hair resting against his shoulder, and looked smilingly down upon the troubled young face.

"Yes, Compadre, I know you think it will be quite for the best and I'm sure it would if - if - "

Peggy paused. She hated to say anything uncomplimentary of the person whom the law said she must regard as her aunt.

"Are you prejudiced, my dear?"

There was mild reproof in Dr. Llewellyn's tone.

"I am afraid I am. You see I have been with the 'Little Mother,' and I do love her so, and Polly's mother, too, and oh, Compadre, she is lovely. Perfectly lovely. If you could only see Polly with her. There is something - something in their attitude toward each other which makes me understand just what Mamma and I might have been to each other had she lived. I never guessed what it meant until last winter, or felt it as I did up there in New London. Daddy Neil is dear and precious but Mamma and I would have been just what Polly and HER mother are to each other; I know it."

"Will it not be possible for you and your aunt to grow very deeply attached to one another? She, I understand, is quite alone in the world, and you should mean a great deal to each other."

Peggy's slight form shuddered ever so little in his circling arm. That little shudder conveyed more to Dr. Llewellyn than a volume of words could have done. He knew the sensitive, high-strung girl too well not to comprehend that there must be something in Mrs. Peyton Stewart's personality which grated harshly upon her, and concluded that it would be wiser not to pursue the subject.

"Go for a spin upon Shashai's silky back, and let Tzaritza's long leaps carry yon into a world of gladness. Nelly has been asking for you and the five-mile ride to her home will put things straighter."

"I'll go," answered Peggy, and left him to get into her linen riding skirt, for it was still very warm in Maryland.

From the moment of her return Tzaritza had never left Peggy's side, and her horses, especially Shashai, Roy and Star had greeted her with every demonstration of affection. She now made her way to the paddock intending to take out her favorite, but when she called him the other two came bounding toward her, nozzling, whinnying, begging for her caresses.

"What SHALL I do with all three of you?" cried Peggy. "I can't ride three at once."

"You'll be having one grand time to git shet o' the other two whichever one you DO take; they've been consoling themselves for your absence by stickin' together as thick as thieves: Where one goes, there goes 'tothers," laughed Shelby, who had gone down to the paddock with her.

"Then let them come along if they want to," and Peggy joined in the laugh.

"You couldn't lose 'em if you tried; first they love you, and then they're so stuck on each other you'd think it was one body with a dozen legs."

Without another word Peggy sprang to Shashai's back. Then with the clear whistle her pets knew so well, was off down the road. That was a mad, wild gallop but when she came to Nelly's home her cheeks were glowing and her eyes shining as of old.

"Oh, HAVE you seen Pepper and Salt?" was almost the first question Nelly asked.

"Well, I guess I have, and aren't they wonders? Oh, I'm so glad I saw them that day. Do you know they are to be entered in the horse-show and the steeple-chase this fall? Well, they are. Shelby has made them such beauties. But now tell me all about yourself. I'm going to write to Polly tonight and she will never forgive me if I don't tell her just everything. You are looking perfectly fine. And how is the knee?"

"Just as well as its mate. I wouldn't know I had ever been lame. Your doctor is a wonder, Miss Peggy, and he was so kind. He said you told him you had adopted me and he was bound to take extra good care of me because I was YOUR girl now. I didn't know you had told him to attend me until after you had gone away and I can't thank you enough, but father is so worried because he thinks he will never be able to pay such a bill as Doctor Kendall's ought to be for curing me. But I tell him it will come out all right, just as it always has before, for things are looking up right smart on the farm now. Tom and Jerry certainly do earn their keep, as Mr. Shelby said they would, and they are so splendid and big and round and roly-poly, and strong enough to pull up a tree, father says. Don't you want to come and see them?"

"Indeed I do," and following the beaming, healthy girl whose once pale cheeks were now rounded and rosy, Peggy walked to the stump lot just beyond the little cottage where she was heartily greeted by Jim Bolivar, who said:

"Well, if it ain't a sight fit ter chirker up a dead man ter see ye back again, Miss Peggy. Will you shake hands with me, miss? It's a kind o' dirty and hard hand but it wants ter hold your little one jist a minute ter try ter show ye how much the man it belongs ter thinks of ye."

Peggy laid her own pretty little hand in Jim Bolivar's, saying:

"I wish I could make you understand how glad I am to shake hands with you, and it always makes me so happy to have people like me. It hurts if they don't, you know."

"Well, you ain't likely ter be hurt none ter speak of; no, you ain't, little girl, an' that's a fact. God bless ye! And look at Nelly. Ain't she a clipper? My, things is jist a hummin' on the little old farm now, an' 'fore ye know it we'll be buildin' a piazzy. Now come 'long an' see Tom and Jerry."

And so from one to another went the little chatelaine of Severndale, welcomed at every turn, cheery, helpful, sunny, beloved yet, oh, so lonely in her young girlhood.

And thus passed the first days of Peggy's return to Severndale. Then the eventful one of Mrs. Stewart's arrival dawned. It was a gloriously sunny one; cool from a shower during the previous night. Mrs. Stewart would arrive at five in the afternoon. All morning Peggy had been busy looking to the preparations for her aunt's reception. Harrison had followed out her young mistress' orders to the letter, for somehow of late, Harrison had grown to defer more and more to "Miss Peggy," though secretly, she was not in the least favorably inclined toward the prospective addition to the household: Mammy's report had not tended to pre-dispose her in the lady's favor.

Nevertheless, she was a guest, and a guest at Severndale stood for more than a mere word of five letters.

Peggy ordered the surrey to meet the five P. M. car but chose to ride Shashai, and when Jess set forth with the perfectly appointed carriage and span, Peggy, in her pretty khaki habit fox-trotted beside Comet and Meteor, Tzaritza, as usual, bounding on ahead.

They had gone possibly half the distance when a mad clatter of hoof-beats caused her to exclaim:

"Oh, Jess, they have leaped the paddock fence!"

"Dey sho' has, honey-chile. Dey sho' has," chuckled Jess. " Dat lady what's a-comin' gwine get a 'ception at 'tention what mak' her open her eyes."

"Oh, but I did not want her to have such a welcome. She will think we are all crazy down here," protested Peggy.

"Well, if she think FIVE thoroughbreds tu'ned out fer ter welcome her stan fer crazy folks she gwine start out wid a mistake. Dem hawses gwine mind yo' an' mak' a showin' she ain' gwine see eve'y day of her life lemme tell yo'."

But there was no time to discuss the point further, for Silver Star and Roy came bounding up on a dead run, manes and tails waving, and with the maddest demonstrations of joy at having won out in their determination NOT to be left behind. They rushed to Peggy's side, whinnying their "Hello! How are you?" to Shashai, who answered with quite as much abandon. And then came the transformation: At a word from Peggy they fell into stride beside her and finished the journey to the little depot in as orderly a manner as perfectly trained dogs. When they reached it Peggy stationed them in line, and slipping from Shashai's back ordered Tzaritza to "guard." Then she stepped upon the platform to meet the incoming car, just as little less than a year before she had stepped upon it to welcome the ones whom during that year she had learned to love so dearly, and who had so completely altered her outlook upon life, and who were destined to change and - yes - save her future, just as surely as the one now momentarily drawing nearer and nearer was destined to bring a crisis into it.

The car came buzzing up to the station. There was a flutter of drapery, as a lady with a white French poodle, snapping and snarling at the world at large, and the brakeman in particular, into whose arms it was thrust, descended from the steps.

"Handle Toinette carefully. Dear me, you are crushing her, the poor darling. Here, porter, take this suitcase," were the commands issued.

"I ain't no po'tah," retorted the negro who had been singled out by Madam. Then he turned and walked off.

"Insolent creature," was the sharp retort, which might have been followed by other comments had not Peggy at that moment advanced to meet her aunt. When the negro saw that the new arrival was a friend of the little lady of Severndale his whole attitude changed in a flash. Doffing his cap he ran toward her saying:

"I looks after it fo' YO', Miss Peggy." The accent upon the pronoun was significant.

"Thank you, Sam," was the quick, smiling answer. Then:

"How do you do, Aunt Katharine? Welcome to Severndale," and her hand was extended to welcome her relative, for Peggy's instincts were rarely at fault.

But her aunt was too occupied in receiving Toinette into her protecting embrace to see her niece's hand, and Peggy did not force the greeting. "Will you come to the carriage?" she asked, "I hope you are not very tired from the journey."

"On the contrary, I am positively exhausted. I don't see how you can endure those horrid, smelly little cars. We would not consent to ride a mile in them at home. Is this your carriage? Hold my dog, coachman, while I am getting in," and Toinette was thrust into Jess' hand which she promptly bit, and very nearly had her small ribs crushed for her indiscretion, her yelp producing a cry from her doting mistress.

"Be careful, you stupid man. You can't handle that delicate little thing as though she were one of your great horses. Now put the suitcase by the driver and leave room here beside me for my niece," were the further commands issued to "Sam."

Sam did as ordered, but when a dime was proffered answered:

"Keep yo' cash, lady. I done DAT job fer ma little quality lady hyer, an' SHE pays wid somethin' bettah."

Mrs. Stewart was evidently NOT in her amiable guise, but turning to Peggy she strove to force a smile and say:

"Ignorant creatures, aren't they, dear? But come. I've a thousand questions to ask."

"Thank you, Aunt Katharine, but I rode over on my saddle horse, and shall have to ask you to excuse me."

Not until that moment did Mrs. Stewart notice the three horses standing like statues just beyond the carriage with the splendid dog lying upon the ground in front of them.

Peggy crossed the intervening space and with the one word "Up," to Tzaritza, set her escort in motion. They reached forward long, slim necks to greet her, Tzaritza bounding up to rest her forepaws upon her shoulders and nestle her silky head against Peggy's face, sure of the solicited caress. Then Peggy bounded to Shashai's back, and the little group, wheeling like a flash, led the way from the depot.

"Good heavens and earth! It is quite time someone came down here to look after that child. I had no idea she was leading the life of a wild western cowboy," was the exclamation from the rear seat of the surrey, plainly overheard by Jess, and, later duly reported.

"Huh, Um," he muttered.

The ride to Severndale held no charm for Madam Stewart. She was too intent upon "that child's mad, hoydenish riding. Good heavens, if such were ever seen in New York," New York with its automaton figures jigging up and down in the English fashion through Central Park being her criterion for the world in general.

Presently beautiful Severndale was reached. Dr. Llewellyn was waiting upon the terrace to greet his ward's aunt, which he did in his stately, courtly manner, but before ten words were spoken he comprehended all Neil Stewart meant in his letter by the words:

"Stand by Peggy. I've landed her up against it," and as the young girl led her aunt into the house, with Mammy, all immaculate dignity following in their wake, he mentally commented: "I fear he HAS made a grave mistake; a very grave one, but Providence ordereth all things and we see darkly. It may be one of the 'wondrous ways.' We must not form our conclusions too hastily. No, not too hastily."

And just here we must leave Peggy Stewart upon the threshold of a new world the entrance to which is certainly not enticing. What the experiences of that month were, and the revelations which came into Peggy's life during it; how the perplexing problem was solved and who helped to solve it, must be told in the story of Peggy Stewart at School. But just now we must leave her doing her best to make "Aunt Katharine" comfortable; to smooth out some of the kinks already making a snarl of the usually evenly ordered household, for Mammy had not changed her opinion one particle, and when Harrison went back to her own undisputed realm of the big house she was overheard to remark:

"Well, Neil Stewart is a man, so OF COURSE, he's bound to do some fool things, but unless I miss MY guess, he's played his trump card THIS time."